THE DAY I WAS ERASED

ALSO BY
LISA THOMPSON

THE
GOLDFISH
BOY

THE
LIGHT
JAR

THE DAY I WAS

ERASED

LISA THOMPSON

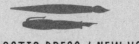

SCHOLASTIC PRESS / NEW YORK

First published in the United Kingdom in 2019 by Scholastic UK
Ltd., Euston House, 24 Eversholt Street, London NW1 1DB.

The publisher does not have any control over and does
not assume any responsibility for author or third-party
websites or their content.

Library of Congress Cataloging-in-Publication Data available

ISBN 978-1-338-58956-6

10 9 8 7 6 5 4 3 2 1   20 21 22 23 24
Printed in the U.S.A.   23

First US edition, June 2020

Book design by Christopher Stengel

FOR DAD

CHAPTER 1
GARBAGE

My dog, Monster, is the best in the world: FACT.

Dad says he's probably half dog, half mole because he's so good at digging tunnels: mainly underneath our garden fence. He's really round, so it's a miracle he doesn't get stuck.

I watched him do it once. He sat on the flower bed and stared at the wooden panels, as if he was trying to work out how to tackle them, and then he began to dig. Dirt flew from under his wagging tail, and then he did this weird shuffling-along-on-his-stomach thing with his back legs flattened on either side. The next second he was gone.

When he escapes, he always heads to the same place: Mrs. Banks's front garden. He charges at her garbage cans, knocks them over, and then, like a big, furry vacuum cleaner, gobbles everything up. And I mean *everything*. He threw up a pair of underwear onto the living room carpet once, and Mum wasn't sure if she should wash them and take them back to Mrs. Banks. I pointed out that if they were in the garbage in the first place, then she obviously didn't want them, did she?

Mrs. Banks caught Monster going through her garbage for the third time this week. She arrived on our doorstep with him tucked backward under her arm. His tail was wagging around and around, like it does when he's happy, and she had to put her head to one side to stop it from hitting her in the face.

"You do realize that this animal is completely out of control, don't you, Mrs. Beckett?" she said. Mum was a bit flustered because she'd been in the middle of an argument with Dad when she answered the door. Monster stopped wagging and began to wriggle, but the more he wriggled the more Mrs. Banks gripped on to him.

"He's been going through my trash again. *And* he left a 'present' on my lawn."

"A present?" said Mum, rubbing her forehead.

"Yes, Mrs. Beckett. A present. The foul, smelly, disgusting kind."

Monster's tail wagged again as if he were showing us all where the "present" had come from. I snorted and Mrs. Banks shot a look at me. There was a high-pitched yelp as she tightened her grip around my dog even more.

"You shouldn't be holding him like that!" I shouted. "He doesn't like it. You let him go right now, you mean old . . . cow!"

"Maxwell!" said Mum.

Mrs. Banks's eyes went so wide I thought they were going to fall out of her head.

"Are you going to let your son . . . your *child* talk to me in that way?"

Mum looked at me and opened her mouth, but nothing came out. It was as if she didn't have a clue what to say. Monster's tail had stopped wagging now and he began to whine. I jumped off our step and tried to grapple him out of Mrs. Banks's arms.

"You're hurting him! Let go of him! Let go of him now!"

Mrs. Banks let out a squeal. "Oh! Get off! Get off me, you . . . you horror!"

"Maxwell! What has come over you?" cried Mum, pulling me

back by my shoulder. Monster dropped to the ground with a yelp. He gave himself a quick shake, then trotted inside as if nothing had happened.

"I'm so sorry, Mrs. Banks. Maxwell isn't usually like this."

Mrs. Banks swept her hair out of her face.

"I beg to differ, Mrs. Beckett. Your son is a beast. I know it, the school knows it, and I'm pretty sure *you* know it. I suggest you get that dog *and your son* under control, or I'll inform the authorities."

She turned on her heel and stormed off down the pathway and through the space in the wall where the gate used to be. Mum closed the door, taking a deep breath. I knew she was about to have a go at me, but Dad started yelling from the kitchen.

"Amanda?! Have you been eating my chicken pasta? Taking the Post-it off doesn't mean it's yours!"

Mum gritted her teeth, then stomped down the hallway.

"No, Eddie! I haven't touched your flipping pasta!"

I huffed. My parents had this stupid arrangement where they each bought their own food and put Post-its on what was theirs. If they thought the other one had eaten something that didn't belong to them, they went nuts. My sister, Bex, and I didn't use labels; we just ate whatever Mum or Dad cooked for us. I hated those Post-its. I hated them nearly as much as I hated Mrs. Banks for hurting my dog.

Mum and Dad had a massive fight that night. One of their worst. I was trying to go to sleep, but I could hear them through the bedroom wall shouting at each other.

I wanted to go into Bex's room and sit it out with her, like we used to do during a thunderstorm when we were little. Bex would never let me in her room now, though. She's fifteen and a total nerd. She's even got a poster on her wall with the names of all the kings and queens of England on it. I mean, who does that? Why doesn't she have a pop group or a film star or something a *normal* fifteen-year-old girl would have? Still, I'd rather have been in her room than on my own listening to them argue.

Mum and Dad shouted about Monster and Mrs. Banks and then turned to me. They were blaming each other for all the trouble I kept getting into at school. I wrapped my pillow around my head and tried to doze off until finally, at about midnight, I heard the front door slam. I sat up and listened as Dad's van started and sped off down the road. I relaxed a bit then. Dad just drives around until he's calmed down, and he comes home when we're all asleep.

I pulled the blanket over my head and curled up into a ball. If Mrs. Banks hadn't knocked with Monster under her arm, then there wouldn't have been all that shouting. It was all Mrs. Banks's fault. As I drifted off to sleep, I thought of a way to get my revenge.

CHAPTER 2
FLAMINGO

The pink flamingo on Mrs. Banks's lawn was looking at me funny. Its black, staring eye didn't move as I crouched down in the corner of the garden.

I walked past Mrs. Banks's house every day on my way to and from school. She lives next door to my friend Reg, and the tall plastic flamingo had appeared beside her pond about a month ago. Mrs. Banks was in her garden most days, admiring the flamingo or moving it into a slightly different position. I wouldn't be surprised if she actually talked to it. Well, that stupid bird was going to get it.

A prickly bush beside me began to shake, and a wet nose emerged from the undergrowth and sniffed the air.

"Monster! How did you get out again? Keep down. She'll skin you alive if she gets ahold of you, you do know that, don't you?" Monster head-butted me on my side and I rubbed his neck. His bottom wiggled madly as his tail propelled itself around and around.

I stared back at the flamingo and held on to a half piece of brick I'd found in our back garden.

"Who would buy something so ugly, Monster? That flamingo is the most disgusting thing I've ever seen." He licked the back of my hand and I wiped the stringy, sticky goo onto my school trousers. "In fact, the whole garden is hideous," I said. "Look at it!"

There were stepping stones from the front gate to the door so there was no risk that any visitor would walk on her precious grass. Not that I'd ever known her to have visitors. No one called at Mrs. Banks's house for a cup of tea or to see how she was doing. However, plenty of people stopped as they walked by to gawk at the garden. Not because it was beautiful or full of tropical plants or anything, but because it was so . . . *cheesy*. Dotted among the bright-colored flowers were a family of concrete squirrels wearing top hats, seven pixies in various gymnastic poses, an old man with a big fat tummy pushing a tiny wheelbarrow, and a plastic wishing well. The pink flamingo was her latest purchase, and only this morning I'd watched her wipe some invisible dirt off it as I walked to school. It was clearly her new favorite thing.

I held tightly on to the brick and looked at the windows of Mrs. Banks's bungalow. She had blinds in her windows like the ones you get in offices—the vertical kind, in a horrible, dirty green color. They were all closed.

"Right. Are you ready for this?" I said. Monster did a deep sigh next to me, then began to lick his butt. He always does that when he gets bored.

"Okay," I said as I stood up. "Three, two, one . . ." I twisted the brick around in my hand, then took a shot . . .

Now, what I'd intended to do was quite different from what actually happened. What I'd *intended* to do was to knock the bird over and maybe give it a bit of a dent in its stupid plastic head. It might not sound like much, but for Mrs. Banks, finding her brand-new flamingo lying on her perfect lawn would have been enough to send her into a total meltdown.

But what actually happened was this:

The piece of brick flew out of my hand and spun around as it hurtled toward the bacon-pink bird. I watched with my mouth open as I waited for it to reach its target. And reach it, it most certainly did. It not only hit the flamingo, it took its head clean off with one almighty CRACK!

The plastic head somersaulted into the air and landed on Mrs. Banks's doorstep like some sick parcel delivery. The decapitated body stayed exactly where it was, its skinny legs still rooted into the ground.

"Oops," I whispered. I slowly backed away toward the low fence. The vertical blinds began to twitch.

"Come on, Monster. We'd better run," I said. I grabbed my school bag and clambered over the fence while my dog tried to squeeze through a tiny gap. He'd managed to get in that way, but now he was struggling to fit through. He was stuck.

"Pull yourself, Monster!" I said as he just stood there, wagging his tail at me. "We've gotta go!"

I was about to jump back over the fence and push his rear through when he did one more strain and burst out onto the pavement. He gave himself a shake, then looked up at me as if to say, "Right. What next?"

I began to laugh as we ran. A headless flamingo! Right there in her garden! It couldn't have gone better. She would probably explode from anger. She'd open her front door, see the head lying there on her doormat, and erupt like a fiery volcano. We turned the corner and slowed to a walk as we got closer to home.

"We'd better keep our heads down for a bit now. Just in case she suspects. She's going to be *so* mad," I said.

I turned up our garden path and let myself in, throwing my bag on the stairs and kicking the door shut behind me. Monster trotted off to the kitchen to check if anything had appeared in his food bowl.

"Mum? The printer's run out of ink and I need to get my project . . . Oh, it's you." My sister, Bex, appeared at the top of the stairs. She crossed her arms. "Have you been in a fight again? Mum'll go mad."

I looked down at my school uniform. My shirt was hanging out of my trousers and ripped at the side where I'd caught it on Mrs. Banks's fence. My shoes were brown from mud, rather than the regulation black, and my tie was wrapped around my left wrist. I hated wearing a tie. All in all, I looked pretty normal.

"You do know you'll be grounded again, don't you?" said Bex, stomping down the stairs and pushing past me.

"I haven't been in a fight," I said, following her to the kitchen. "I've actually been very busy teaching Mrs. Banks a lesson."

Bex ignored me and began rummaging through the kitchen drawers.

Mum and Dad were both out, so the house was quiet for once. I opened the fridge and tutted when I saw the fluttering of yellow Post-its. There was one with a name written on it attached to nearly every item of food or drink. Some said *Amanda* and some said *Eddie*. On a bottle of white wine there was one Post-it that read: *Amanda's. DO NOT TOUCH THIS UNDER ANY CIRCUMSTANCES.*

I took a bottle of Coke that didn't have a Post-it on it, which meant Bex or I could have it.

"Why don't they just have two fridges? Surely that would be better than all those stupid labels," I said, slamming the door.

"Maxwell, do you have *any* idea where the printer ink cartridges are? I need some urgently," said Bex, opening another drawer.

I took a big swig of Coke. "Oh yeah! I do, actually," I said.

Bex turned to me. "Fantastic! Where are they?"

I took another gulp, held up my hand, and then:

"YURRRPPPP."

I let out the loudest belch I could. Bex huffed.

"You are a disgusting human being. Do you realize that, Maxwell Beckett?"

I laughed as I took a bag of chips out of the cupboard. I pulled off the Post-it that said *Eddie* on the front and stuffed it into the garbage. Dad wouldn't mind me eating his chips. It was only when Mum ate them that he had a meltdown. I shoved a handful into my mouth as Bex searched through a cupboard.

"Are there any in your room?" she said. "*Please*, Maxwell. I want to print my Persian Empire project."

I didn't even know what that was, but I was pretty sure it was something she had done "for fun" rather than for homework. Like I said before, my sister is weird.

I pretended to think about where the ink cartridges could possibly be by putting my head to one side and tapping my chin with my finger.

"Let me see . . . I think they might be . . . um . . . No. No idea, I'm afraid," I said, showing her a mouthful of mashed-up chips.

Bex groaned and turned away.

"Urgh, you're so disgusting," she said. "Why were you even born?"

I grinned to myself, then balled up the chip bag and threw it in the trash.

CHAPTER 3
MONSTER

Monster and I have a really special bond. *Really* special. When he's not eating or sleeping or licking his butt, he's usually right beside me, following me around. He'll look up at me with his big brown eyes, and I'm pretty sure he understands that it's because of me that he's alive today. That's right: I, Maxwell Beckett, saved Monster's life.

It all happened on my walk home from school about a year ago. I had detention again, which you could see as a bad thing, but it was actually a good thing because it meant I was in the right place at the right time. I'd had a lot of detentions that term already: for talking back to the teachers, wearing the wrong uniform, not doing my homework, setting off a fire alarm, and telling everyone that Charlie Geek was moving to Dubai. I was so convincing on that one that he got called to the principal's office to be asked why his mum hadn't spoken to the school about it. Charlie's my best friend, and although he got a bit upset to start with, he found it funny in the end. I *think* he did, anyway. For this particular detention, I was kept behind because I'd put the class's math books in the cafeteria trash can—which was a lot easier to do than you'd think . . .

After math (which was probably all about angles or something else that was a complete waste of time), the bell rang and Mr. Gupta told us to put our books on his desk on our way out so that he could mark our homework.

I hadn't done mine. And I hadn't done it the week before, either. Not doing my homework wouldn't usually bother me, but I knew that this time it would mean a phone call home to Mum and Dad. And that would mean another big argument. But as I put my book on the top of the pile, there was a CRASH in the corridor. Mr. Gupta rushed out to see what had happened, and I was the last one left in the room. Without really thinking about it, I grabbed all the books and stuffed them into my bag.

The corridor was chaos. One of the science teachers had dropped a tray of jars and test tubes, and there was glass everywhere. Mr. Gupta helped the teacher pick up the pieces while Charlie Geek took it upon himself to form a "human shield" to stop anyone walking through it.

"Stand back, everyone! There's glass. GLASS!" he shouted, like it was an unexploded bomb or something. He's a bit of an idiot sometimes.

I worked out that I had approximately three minutes to get rid of the books and make it to my next lesson, so I legged it to the cafeteria, where they have the biggest garbage cans. In just over seventy-five minutes, everyone would be scraping their lunch plates all over the books, and Mr. Gupta would never know I hadn't done my homework. Perfect.

There were four lunch ladies in the kitchen. One of them was singing opera, badly, and they were all too busy laughing to notice me or the THUD of the books landing in the bottom of the trash can. I grabbed a few paper napkins that were on the side by the cutlery and threw them on top so the books couldn't be seen. I then ran to Geography and was in my seat before the teacher had even looked up from her desk. Easy.

I don't know how I managed to get caught for dumping the books. One of those beady-eyed lunch ladies must have noticed. Mrs. Lloyd, our principal, summoned me to her office during last period and told me the good news: a week of detention and a phone call to my parents. My whole plan to try and avoid any more arguments at home had totally backfired.

After my last day of detention, I decided to take a longer walk home to avoid the shouting while I could. I took a detour down Palmerston Avenue and saw that there was something lying in the road. At first I thought it was an old fur coat, but then it moved. It was a dog! It had long brown ears, a white body, and black and brown patches on its back and legs. It was panting, and its chestnut-colored eyes looked all watery. There were no cars coming so I stepped out into the street.

"Hello, boy," I said, 'cause he wasn't called Monster yet. "Are you hurt?"

The dog slapped his lips together and swallowed and then started licking one of his back paws. He didn't have a collar on, and the fur around his foot was dark with blood. He tried to get up, but as soon as he put his foot onto the pavement, he whined.

"It's your paw, isn't it?" I said. "Have you hurt it?"

I don't know why I was talking to him. I think I was probably trying to keep him calm like they do on those ambulance emergency programs on TV. I was just going to see if I could get him to stand up again when I heard a car. To start with, I wasn't that worried. I waited for the driver to spot me waving my arms and slow down. But the car didn't slow down. In fact, it sped up. If the driver didn't see me soon, then I'd have to jump out of the way and the dog would be flattened like a pancake.

"Hey!" I shouted at the car. "Hey! Slow down! There's an injured animal here!"

The driver was on his phone and looking at himself in his mirror.

"Hey! Get off your phone! Slow down!" I yelled. At the very last second, the driver looked up and swerved around us.

"Stupid idiot!" I screamed after him. I crouched down and the dog swallowed and licked my hand.

"That was a close one," I said. "Right, let's get you home." I scooped him up in my arms, which was pretty hard to do because he was really heavy, and then staggered home.

Now, if you're ever thinking of walking for half a mile while carrying a chubby dog with a bad paw, then I'd suggest you think again. It wasn't easy. And although he seemed quite happy about being carried, his breath stank and he kept licking the side of my face.

"I don't mean to be rude," I huffed. "But . . . you know . . . you might want to . . . lay off some of the treats. You're not a dog—you're a monster." I smiled to myself.

"Yeah, Monster. That's who you are," I said.

When I got home, I put him on the kitchen table, which probably wasn't the best thing to do. Mum hit the roof.

"What were you thinking, bringing a strange dog home,

Maxwell? And putting him on the table like that—he could have rabies! He could be vicious and have a nasty bite!"

The dog looked up at us both, then gave a huge sigh and let off a fart so loud the table shuddered. I snorted but Mum just looked horrified.

"I couldn't leave him there, Mum. He would have died. There was a man on his phone and he drove at us really fast without spotting us and . . ."

Mum gasped.

"Do you mean to tell me that you were standing in the middle . . . *of a road*?! Do you have no sense of danger, Maxwell?"

I rubbed the top of the dog's head.

"Yes . . . but . . . look at him, Mum. He would have *died*."

Mum came over and looked at the dog. He blinked a few times. It was like he was fluttering his long eyelashes at her.

"Well, we can't afford vet bills, so we'd better find out where he comes from and get him back to where he belongs." She picked up the home phone and went off to the living room.

I pulled up a chair and sat beside him. With my head on my hand, I gently stroked his velvety-soft ears.

"She's not always like this," I told him. "She's just a bit stressed at the moment."

Bex walked into the kitchen reading one of her boring books and stopped when she saw us.

"Urgh. What is that?" she said, grimacing.

"He's called Monster," I said as the dog began to lick my hand. "I saved his life."

Bex raised her eyebrows and then walked back out again. She never really says a lot with her mouth, my sister, but she can really say a lot with the rest of her face.

When Dad got home from work, he told me we could take the dog to the vet in the back of his van.

"Go and get a blanket from your room, Maxwell. Something nice and soft. And maybe a pillow as well?" he said.

I'd not known Dad to be particularly keen on dogs, but because Mum was all stressed about having Monster in the house, he suddenly acted like he was some kind of expert, just to annoy her.

The vet said the dog didn't have a microchip so, at the moment, there was no way of knowing who his owner was. He thought he was quite old (the dog, not the owner) and he said he was a breed called a beagle and that they had a tendency to put on weight.

"This chap is a perfect example," he said, ruffling the dog's ears. "Had a few too many burgers, haven't you, old boy?"

The beagle smacked his lips together as if he knew what the word *burgers* meant. The vet took a good look at his injured back paw and then got some tweezers and pulled out a lump of glass.

"This is why he didn't want to put his foot down. I'll just clean up the wound and put something over it to keep any infection out."

While he did this, he and Dad talked about what to do next. The vet said he'd call the local authority, who would come and collect the dog. They'd put him in a nearby animal shelter to give the owner a chance to come forward for him.

"But we could look after him. Couldn't we?" I said.

The vet shook his head.

"That's not the way it works, I'm afraid. If you want to rehome him, then you can register an interest with the shelter. They'll have to come and visit your home and make sure you're ready to take on a dog. If he's not claimed, then potentially you'll be able to keep him."

My stomach flipped at the idea. My very own dog!

The vet said there was no charge so, on our way out, Dad put some money in a charity collection tin that they had at reception.

"Don't get your hopes up, Maxwell. Even if the owners don't claim him, we'll have to get your mum to agree. And you know how awkward she can be sometimes."

I didn't say anything. I hated it when one of my parents did that, trying to get me to be horrible about the other one.

When we got home I told Mum that we might be able to keep the dog and, surprisingly, Mum was okay about it. I think it was to annoy Dad, but at least they both agreed.

During the week, a woman from the shelter came to inspect our house while I was at school. The woman said that we'd definitely be able to rehome Monster, providing his owner didn't claim him. Mum told me not to get my hopes up, but I couldn't help feeling really excited.

We visited him in the shelter one day. They had put a *Reserved* sticker on his cage so that if his owner didn't come forward, then he could come to live with us. Mum laughed and said that it was pretty unlikely anyone else would be interested in a smelly old beagle. Monster didn't seem to mind and he wagged his tail at us from inside his cage.

After two weeks and no sign of the owner, Monster was ours. I couldn't believe it! I actually had my own dog! And not any old dog, either—a dog that I'd saved! I went to the shelter to collect him with Dad, and when we got home, I carried him across the threshold as if he was too important to walk, even though his paw was pretty much healed now.

Mum had made him a little bed in the corner of the kitchen by the garbage cans, with a dish of water beside it. Dad started fussing, saying that if we let the dog sleep there, he'd get a draft from under the door, but Mum said it was the best place because we didn't want him to overheat. Monster's head went back and forth, watching my parents as they argued.

"You'll learn to ignore them. They'll stop eventually," I whispered in his ear as I put him down in his bed. Mum and Dad moved to the living room. They'd finished arguing about the dog and had moved on to money. After me, this was their favorite subject to fight about.

"If you hadn't wasted all that money on that skiing trip, maybe you'd have a deposit for an apartment. Have you even considered that?" screamed Mum.

"Fine, Amanda. Well, let's just add up all those hairdressing appointments you've had over the last year and see what that comes to, shall we?"

I went to the fridge and took out some ham. I took off the Post-it that said *Amanda* on it, then sat beside Monster and hand-fed him. Before long, the shouting became just like background noise and I barely even noticed it.

CHAPTER 4
CHARLIE

"Charlie! Hey! Charlie! Wait up!"

I could see Charlie Geek about fifty yards in front of me as I walked to school. I could recognize his walk anywhere—it was more of a stumble, like he was about to fall over.

"Charlie!" I said, whacking him on the arm as I caught up to him. "Didn't you hear me? I've been yelling at you for ages." Then I spotted the white headphones in his ears.

"Maxwell!" he said, pulling out an earbud. "You've got to listen to this." He fumbled as he tried to put it in my ear, but I took it from him and did it myself.

We stood there for a moment, Charlie grinning widely as I listened. It sounded like the inner workings of a washing machine.

"Great. So, what's this one, then? Don't tell me. Is it . . . is it the small intestine of a blue whale?"

Charlie stared at me.

"Can you get audio of that?"

I rolled my eyes.

"I dunno, Charlie. You'd know more about that than me."

Charlie glazed over for a moment as he thought about it, and then he shook himself back.

"This, my friend," he said, all dramatically, "is the sound of . . . *the sun.*"

I laughed.

"What do you mean, it's the sun?"

We walked onto the school grounds wearing one earbud each.

"Scientists recorded the sounds produced by the magnetic field in the outer atmosphere of the sun. And this is the sound the sun makes. Isn't it brilliant?"

He beamed at me. It just sounded like some random wishy-washy noise to me.

"How long is it?" I asked.

Charlie stared down at his phone.

"I've made a loop of it, so it's about two hours."

He pressed play and smiled for a second, but then his head suddenly jolted backward as someone slammed right into him. The earbuds pinged out of our ears.

"Oops, sorry! Didn't see you there, Charlie Geek."

Marcus Grundy walked past us, his teeth gritted in a false smile.

"That's all right, Marcus. No problem," said Charlie, rubbing the back of his neck as Marcus disappeared into the crowd.

"What did you say that for?!" I said. "He shoved you deliberately!"

Charlie blinked at me a few times as he put his earbuds back in his ears.

"I don't think so, Maxwell," he said, screwing the little buds in tighter. "I WAS OBVIOUSLY IN HIS WAY."

He shouted the last bit because he couldn't hear himself talking over his stupid sun noises. A few people turned and stared, and I tried to walk on without him, but he grabbed me by the shoulder.

"ARE YOU GOING TO COME TO SCIENCE CLUB THIS AFTERNOON, MAXWELL? LIKE YOU SAID YOU WOULD?"

I waved my hand at him, trying to get him to keep his voice down. A girl in Bex's year, Claudia Bradwell, strutted over.

"Ah . . . you going to science club with your special friend, are you, Maxwell? You trying to be a nerdy nerd like your boring sister?"

She strutted off before I got a chance to answer back. Her group of friends fluttered behind her, scrolling on their phones. I couldn't stand Claudia Bradwell. She'd given my sister a really hard time.

I looked at Charlie, who was, as always, oblivious to anything that was going on around him. He pulled his stupid duck face, which he always did to try and make me laugh. When he saw I wasn't smiling, his face dropped.

"You are coming, aren't you? You promised!" Last week he'd persuaded me that science club might actually be interesting because you got to do cool things like blow stuff up, but there was no way I was going now.

I ignored him and walked off, but I could hear him shuffling behind me trying to keep up. We'd been friends since we were small, but everyone knew he was a total nerd. Charlie Geek isn't even his real name. His real name is Charlie Kapoor. I made up the name Charlie Geek because he's so . . . geeky. Even some of the teachers call him that and, rather than get annoyed, he laughs like it's some kind of compliment. He's such an idiot he can't even tell when people are being mean to him.

"Right, come on . . . settle down, 8A. What's the matter with you today?" said my homeroom teacher, Mr. Howard, as we all slouched into class. "Come on! Butts on seats. Maxwell Beckett, that means you . . ."

Charlie rushed in behind me and dived into the seat next to me in case someone else tried to sit there. Which they wouldn't. I didn't look at him.

"Okay . . . so as you are all aware, tomorrow is the school's Hundredth Anniversary Celebration whatsit . . ." said Mr. Howard. There was a general "whoop" from the class.

"Yes, yes . . . I know. The excitement is unbearable," said Mr. Howard, scrunching up his eyes as everyone began to chatter. "Believe me, 8A, when I say, I really . . . can't wait. Really . . ."

I put up my hand. Even I was excited about this one, and usually I'd avoid anything organized by the school.

"Sir! Sir! Sir!"

Mr. Howard perched on the edge of his desk beside me. I had to sit at the front of the class so that he could keep an eye on me.

"Yes, Maxwell?"

"Are you bringing Ms. Huxley, sir? As your date?"

Someone from the back row let out a wolf whistle, and Mr. Howard blushed. He'd been dating the Spanish teacher for nearly a year now, but I still liked to mention it whenever I could, just to see his face change color.

"Yes, Maxwell. Thank you. Ms. Huxley will be there. As will all the teaching staff."

I smiled and leaned back in my chair. It was my doing, the

whole Howard/Huxley romance. If it wasn't for me, they wouldn't be together. Mr. Howard's face slowly returned to its usual shade, and I put my hand up again.

"Sir! Sir! Sir!"

Mr. Howard sighed.

"What now, Maxwell?"

"Is it true, sir . . ." I paused for dramatic effect. "Is it true that Jed and Baz are filming their TV roadshow, right here in school tomorrow?"

I winced as every girl and a few boys let out a deafening squeal. Mr. Howard glared at me.

"But . . . how? How did you know about that? That's top secret!"

The screams got even louder when the class realized I hadn't just made it up.

I'd actually known about it for a couple of weeks now, as I'd seen it in our principal's emails. I'd been sent to see Mrs. Lloyd for being rude to my French teacher and was told to wait in her office while she dealt with something going on in reception. While I was waiting, I took a quick peek at her computer screen, which she'd accidentally left unlocked. One of her emails was open and the subject title was: *Confirmation of Filming: The Jed and Baz TV Roadshow.* I read as much of the email as I could. My tummy flipped over. Jed and Baz's roadshow was coming to our school on the night of the Hundredth Anniversary Celebration! They were going to be filming an entire show in our auditorium! I couldn't believe it. Jed and Baz were MASSIVE. Their roadshow was the most popular show on TV at the moment, mainly because they filmed in all sorts of weird places, like in someone's living room or on a beach or at an amusement park. And it was always a secret as to where they were going to turn up next. They were *soooo* funny and they had live music and amazing competitions where you could win free vacations and cars and stuff. And they were coming to *our* school!! I sat back in my seat just before Mrs. Lloyd came walking in, and I tried not to grin too much while she gave me a lecture. I left the office that day and managed to keep the news to myself until right about now. The reaction from my class was everything I'd hoped for: hysteria.

Mr. Howard walked around the class, waving his arms up and down and saying, *"SSHHHHHH!"* with such force he left a spray of spit as he went.

"Okay . . . Okay, 8A. Let's have a bit of calm, shall we? Yes . . . so you all knew there was something special planned for tomorrow evening, and now it seems that surprise has been totally ruined. Hasn't it, Maxwell?"

I shrugged. Everyone was too excited to be bothered.

"I don't know how you came across this information, which was, until now, highly classified, but I suggest you stop sharing things. Okay? You've had twenty-nine negative points this month already and multiple detentions. And as I understand it, if you get one more negative, then you'll be excluded from the ball—is that right?"

I heard Charlie gasp beside me as I nodded.

"Right. So, keep your head down and stay out of trouble. Do you think you can manage that?"

Mr. Howard walked away without waiting for an answer.

He was right. My parents had received a letter stating that if I continued to misbehave, then I would be given a thirtieth negative point and I wouldn't be allowed to attend the ball tomorrow night.

"You'd better be careful, Maxwell. You don't want to miss Jed and Baz and the chance to get on TV," whispered Charlie.

I snorted.

"I won't. And anyway, they won't stop me from going to the ball after everything *I've* done for the school."

The school owed me big-time for a competition I'd won back in sixth grade. I crossed my arms and Charlie pulled a face.

He didn't look so sure.

CHAPTER 5
TENNIS

The bell rang and Charlie and I got up and made our way to our first class, which was PE. It was my favorite subject and Charlie's worst. I'd missed a lot of sports lessons this term for mucking about, but in the last couple of weeks, I'd been allowed back in the class again. Mrs. Allen, the teacher, had started teaching us how to play tennis, and we all stood around her on the court with our rackets ready. I kept spinning mine on its head, but she gave me a stern look, so I stopped.

"Remember what we learned last week, 8A: The key to holding your racket correctly is to feel like you are shaking someone's hand," said Mrs. Allen. "Now get into pairs, hold the racket out for your partner, and let them find the correct grip."

I could see Charlie making his way toward me. We always stuck together in PE because, basically, no one else wanted to be with either of us. I messed around too much and Charlie was just useless. He couldn't even catch a ball. He grinned at me and held a racket out for me to "shake." I was getting fed up being stuck with him all the time; he was such a doughnut. I snatched the racket away from him.

"Oww. No need to be so rough, Maxwell," he said, rubbing his hand. "Now hold out yours."

I huffed and pointed the racket handle toward him, but every time he went to take it, I moved it away. His reflexes were so slow, there was no way he was going to get ahold of it.

"Oh, now . . . come on, Maxwell," he said, laughing. I kept moving the racket so it was just out of his reach. He frowned and tried to second-guess which way I was going to go, but he was wrong every single time.

"Are you trying to work out a scientific calculation, Charlie?" I said as I darted the racket left and right. "Come on, there must be some formula or something that you can compute in that big brain of yours."

Charlie wasn't laughing anymore, and his face was running with sweat. He was snorting through his nose, his eyes fixed on the racket handle.

"That's enough, Maxwell," shouted Mrs. Allen from across the court. I paused for a moment but started again as soon as she'd turned around.

"Come on, Charlie. You can do it!" said a girl named Amy Branford. A few others saw something was going on and wandered over. I kept darting the racket from side to side, up and down, and Charlie failed to grab it every time.

"Concentrate!" said Marcus Grundy. "Try and work out which way he's going to go."

Charlie stopped for a moment and looked at him. Marcus Grundy was giving him advice? I couldn't believe it, either.

"Well, go on then!" said Marcus, chewing on the side of his thumb.

Charlie went to grab the racket and I quickly moved it again.

"Ooooh, you nearly got it!" squealed Tabitha Wright.

Everyone was watching. Mrs. Allen was busy moving a basket of balls over to the opposite end of the courts. Someone began a slow clap and the others joined in.

"Char-lie! Char-lie! Char-lie!"

I could see Mrs. Allen turn and start making her way over with her hands on her hips.

"Come on, you can do it!"

"Just grab it, Charlie!"

"Don't let him beat you!"

I couldn't believe it—they were *all* on his side!

"What is going on here?" boomed Mrs. Allen, and the chanting fizzled out.

I turned around and Charlie reached for the racket and yanked it out of my hand. The crowd went crazy, cheering and clapping.

"But . . . but I'd stopped!" I shouted. "He didn't get it fairly—he just grabbed it when I stopped!"

"Face it, Maxwell. You're a *loser*," said Marcus, inches from my face.

"Yeah, he won it fair and square," said Sanjeev Howe.

Charlie was grinning, clutching his racket to his chest as everyone applauded and patted him on the back.

"That didn't count!" I yelled again.

I went to take the racket away from him, but he was hugging it like it was his precious teddy bear.

"Let go, Charlie, and we can have another go, yeah? Best of three?" I said.

I didn't want to be humiliated, especially by him.

"That's enough now," said Mrs. Allen, but I kept wrestling. "I said that's enough! Everyone get back into your pairs!"

Charlie's hands were gripped tightly around the racket and I tried to pry his fingers off, one by one.

"Get off me!" he said.

"Maxwell Beckett, if you don't leave Charlie alone this very minute, you'll be getting the biggest negative point you can possibly imagine!"

I looked around at Mrs. Allen. Her eyes were bulging and her nostrils were flared. Everyone was silent, waiting to see what I'd do next. I could hear Charlie sniffling behind me. Mrs. Allen walked over to him and put a hand on his shoulder.

"Come on, Charlie. Let's get you paired up with someone else, shall we?"

I couldn't believe it. I'd even lost Charlie as a partner. Everyone was looking at me with disgust in their eyes. Mrs. Allen put Charlie with Kelly Matterson and Tabitha Wright. Kelly put her arm around him and whispered something that made him laugh. I tried to look casual about it, but there was clearly no one left to pair up with me. As they all started shaking hands with their rackets again, I walked toward the basket on long legs and gave it a great big kick. The basket came crashing down, and hundreds of yellow tennis balls cascaded out and bounced around the court.

"Maxwell Beckett! Pick those all up, right now!" screamed Mrs. Allen.

I huffed and slowly walked toward the balls that were rolling around. At least it gave me something to do now that I didn't have a partner.

"Okay, everyone," said Mrs. Allen. "I want you to grab a ball and practice bouncing it up and down on your racket, like so . . ." Mrs. Allen demonstrated, and then everyone rushed over and grabbed a ball from the floor.

I looked over at Charlie and watched him. He couldn't even keep the ball on the flat racket, let alone hit it up and down. If he'd been partnered with me, I'd have gotten frustrated and shouted at him to do it properly. Now that he was surrounded by the rest of the class, who suddenly thought he was brilliant, he looked like he was having a great time.

"Maxwell, come on. Those balls aren't going to put themselves in the basket," yelled Mrs. Allen as I stood there watching everyone.

Charlie dropped his ball again and lumbered after it, laughing as he went.

I turned away. A ball rolled toward my foot, so I bent down and CRACK. My head smashed against something soft. I looked up and saw Charlie's face. Or, rather, Charlie's hands covering his face.

"Owwwww!!!" he cried. "My nose! My nose!"

I put my hand on his shoulder.

"Sorry! I didn't see you. I was just getting the ball!" I said.

Charlie's eyes peered over the tops of his hands. A gush of blood was pouring down his arm.

"Mrs. Allen! Mrs. Allen!" shouted Kelly. "Maxwell head-butted Charlie!"

Mrs. Allen rushed over.

"I didn't! I didn't mean to!" I shouted. "We just went for the ball at the same time!"

I looked back at Charlie, who was peeking over his hands at me.

"Charlie! Tell them it was an accident. Tell them!"

He took his hands away from his face, his arms now crimson with blood, and then his eyes rolled into the back of his head and he fell to the floor with a great THUD.

CHAPTER 6
BLOOD

I think I'm definitely right when I say that a nosebleed can look a *whole* lot worse than it actually is. But that didn't stop everyone in my class from freaking out.

Mrs. Allen told Adel Barnes to go to the office for help. Adel nodded, rolled up his sleeves, then sprinted off like he was some kind of superhero going to save the world. Charlie was out cold on the ground, his chin rosy-red like he'd just been stuffing his face with a massive bowl of juicy cherries. Mrs. Allen put him into the recovery position, which I think was a bit over the top, to be honest. Someone started crying at that point, and then Marcus piped up: "Is he dead?"

Mrs. Allen stood up.

"No, Marcus. Don't be ridiculous. He's just fainted, that's all. Now, everyone move back. Give him some air . . . He's going to be fine . . ."

Sanjeev started retching and Kelly rubbed his back.

"I didn't do anything wrong, Mrs. Allen. Honestly," I pleaded.

Mrs. Allen was about to say something when Charlie began to groan. She bent down and helped him into a sitting position.

"It's okay, Charlie. You've just knocked your nose and passed out for a minute or two. You're going to be fine."

Charlie blinked a few times as he sat up. The blood was easing off now, and little red crusts were forming around his nostrils.

"You all right, Charlie?" I asked, but he just looked back at me in a dazed way.

Mrs. Lloyd came storming across the playground with Adel skipping behind her. When she arrived, everyone fell silent. Even Sanjeev stopped retching. She looked around at the crowd of kids staring at her and then her finger pointed toward me.

"Maxwell Beckett. My office. NOW."

I sat outside Mrs. Lloyd's door while Mum and Dad talked to her on their own. Normally when I got in trouble, they'd come in after school, so being called in during the day must have meant things were really bad. However, once I got the chance to explain that it wasn't actually my fault, I was sure everything would be okay.

I could see what was going on in reception from where I was sitting. Charlie had a blue flannel hand towel on his nose. He took it off to inspect it, and I couldn't see any more blood. I think he was probably making a bigger fuss about it than he needed to.

"Charlie! Hey! Charlie!" I called across to him. "You've got to tell them it was an accident."

Charlie looked over, his face all confused. The receptionist told me to be quiet, and then Charlie's mum burst through the big glass doors. She went straight to her son and put her hands on his shoulders, holding him still as she inspected his face. She tutted and then tried to smooth his hair down.

"Hey, Charlie! Charlie! At least you get the rest of the day off, eh?" I shouted, giving him a double thumbs-up.

Charlie's mum glared at me and put her arm around him as they stood up.

"I don't want you anywhere near my son ever again, Maxwell Beckett."

I opened my mouth, but nothing came out.

"You keep away from him, do you hear me?" she added.

I was stunned.

"B-but we're friends. Aren't we, Charlie? Who's he going to hang around with if he can't be friends with me?"

Charlie looked at me and then back at his mum. He went to say something, but his mum was twisting him this way and that, trying to put his coat on him like he was a five-year-old.

"Tell her, then, Charlie! Tell her we're still friends!" I shouted. His mum pulled the zip up on the front of his coat, and then he turned to me and shook his head.

"Sorry, Maxwell," he said.

I couldn't believe it.

"FINE!" I bellowed. "I NEVER EVEN LIKED YOU ANYWAY! YOU'RE JUST A NERDY . . . IDIOT!"

I slumped back into the chair just as Mrs. Lloyd's office door opened.

"WHAT ON EARTH IS GOING ON OUT HERE?!" she demanded.

I scuffed my feet against the carpet.

"As if you're not already in enough trouble, eh, Maxwell? Come on in, then. Let's get this over with," she said. I got up really, really slowly and followed her into her office.

There were three chairs in front of her desk. Mum and Dad were sitting apart, so I sat on the one in the middle.

Mrs. Lloyd rolled up the sleeves on her cardigan and leaned her elbows on the desk. It was her "This is serious" pose. I'd seen it many times before.

"So, Maxwell. You obviously know why you're here. I've had a good chat with your parents, and we're all in agreement that your behavior warrants punishment . . ."

More detentions. Great. I slumped down in the seat as far as I could while Mrs. Lloyd continued.

". . . therefore, I'm very disappointed and actually quite sad to have to tell you that you will *not* be welcome at the Hundredth Anniversary Celebration tomorrow evening."

"*What?!*" I yelled, sitting bolt upright. I couldn't believe it! I felt a great lump forming in my throat and I swallowed it away. "B-but Jed and Baz are going to be there! We're going to be on TV!"

She waved her hand at me.

"And that brings me on to the next thing. I understand from Mr. Howard that in homeroom this morning you took it upon yourself to ruin the news of our surprise guests at tomorrow's event. Why would you do that, Maxwell? Why would you want to spoil it for all the others?"

I opened my mouth, but I wasn't sure what to say.

"I . . . I just thought . . . I . . . I . . ." I stuttered. "Anyway, what happened to Charlie was a complete accident. Honestly!"

I looked at Mum and Dad, but they were both staring down at the horrible beige carpet. Mrs. Lloyd carried on.

"We have plenty of witnesses that say you deliberately head-butted Charlie after you'd been teasing him with a tennis racket. I'm afraid it's your word against theirs, and considering your aptitude for getting into trouble, I would say it's quite obvious who is telling the truth here. Wouldn't you?"

I'd sort of lost the thread of what she was saying, but I got the idea. I was in a ton of trouble and I wasn't going to the ball to see Jed and Baz. I wasn't welcome. The teachers didn't want me there, the kids didn't want me there, the parents of the kids didn't want me there. Everybody hated me.

My heart pounded. I was running out of time. I had to do something to change her mind.

"But . . . but . . . what about the competition I won? If it wasn't for me . . . for *my* drawing . . . the school wouldn't have had all the building work done. It's because of me that it all happened!"

Mrs. Lloyd sighed and put her hands together on the desk.

"We will always be incredibly grateful for your competition win, Maxwell. But that was over a year ago now. And frankly, ever since then, you've been getting into more and more trouble. I can't let this go just because you once won a prize. I'm sorry, but there will be no Hundredth Anniversary Celebration for you."

I bit my bottom lip and clenched my fists. I couldn't believe it.

"Your parents are taking you home for the rest of the day," she said, moving some pieces of paper around her desk. "Over the weekend, Maxwell, I want you to think long and hard about your future here at Green Mills High School. Okay? Have a think about the person you have become and whether you'd want to be friends with him."

I wasn't sure what she meant by that, so I just stared down at my feet and pushed my big toe up against the inside of my shoe. It made a little bump. I kept staring at the little bump until she realized I wasn't going to say anything.

Dad cleared his throat.

"Don't worry, Mrs. Lloyd. We'll have a good chat about this at home, and Maxwell will think about all the problems he's caused today. Won't you, Maxwell?"

Mum added her bit: "And we're very grateful that you aren't suspending him. Aren't we, Maxwell?" she said. I ignored them both. They all stood up and shook hands.

And then we left.

CHAPTER 7
REG

When we got home, I went straight through to the kitchen. Monster climbed out of his bed when he saw me, his tail wagging and his tongue dangling out the side of his mouth. I gave him a bone-shaped treat from a plastic tub, and then I went back into the hallway. Mum and Dad were in the living room with the door shut. I stood outside and listened.

"He's clearly unhappy, Eddie. Can't you see it?"

"Of course I *see* it, Amanda. But what on earth do you expect me to do about it?"

"Try talking to him, perhaps? He needs his dad."

"He needs us both! If you weren't always having a go at me, then maybe—"

"Me? Having a go at you? Oh, that's just ridiculous . . ."

I couldn't face being in the house with them arguing again.

"I'm going to see Reg!" I yelled, and I slammed the front door before they could answer.

Reg lived in a bungalow next door to Mrs. Banks's house. I'd been going to see him more and more lately. There was no shouting at Reg's and definitely no arguing. It was just Reg and his tin of cookies and his endless cups of tea.

When I walked past Mrs. Banks's garden, she was standing

on her front lawn next to the headless flamingo. I stuck my hands in my pockets and looked down.

"Are you responsible for this?" she shouted as I walked past. "The trouble with your sort is that there isn't any discipline at home. You're allowed to do exactly what you want, aren't you? Boundaries. That's what you need. Boundaries! Do you hear me?"

I hurried up Reg's path. Normally I'd shout back, but I didn't want to. Not today. I went around the side of the bungalow to the kitchen door, knocked, then unlocked the door and went in. Reg had given me a key years ago.

Reg was standing by the sink doing some washing up. He had his back to me.

"Hello, Reg. Would you like a cup of tea?" I said, walking to the cupboard and getting out two mugs.

Reg turned around, his eyes wide and his soapy hands dripping onto the floor.

"Oh, I'm sorry. Do I know you?" he said, his face confused.

I sighed.

"Yes, Reg. I'm Maxwell. Maxwell Beckett. Remember? I come and see you nearly every single day."

He frowned as he dried his hands on a tea towel.

"Maxwell, you say . . . Maxwell . . . hmmm," he murmured.

I switched the kettle on and put a tea bag in each mug. I got the milk out of the fridge. There wasn't much left.

"You're running out, Reg," I said, giving the carton a little shake. "Do you want me to go and get some for you?" Reg was getting old now and very forgetful.

He took the milk from me.

"You don't want to be doing that." He laughed awkwardly. "We don't even know each other!"

The kettle clicked off, and I poured water into the mugs.

"Come on. I'll show you who I am," I said, putting the kettle back. I held his elbow and guided him into the living room. He stood beside me in front of the fireplace. Resting on the mantelpiece was my portrait of Reg that had come first in a national drawing competition. It was framed and behind glass. I picked it up.

"See this picture of you? I drew it. Remember? I won a big prize for my school."

I held it toward him.

"Look, it says, *Reg by Maxwell Beckett*. That's me. *I'm* Maxwell."

One day I hoped he'd learn to recognize me straightaway, but that day hadn't come yet.

"Maxwell . . . ah yes. I know, I know . . . I know who you are. Of course I do," he said, but I could tell by his face that he didn't. He settled down into his armchair. "Go and get the cookie tin, would you, Maxwell? There's a new pack of snickerdoodles in there."

I went back to the kitchen, finished making the tea, and got the cookie tin out of the cupboard. I put everything on a tray, took it into the living room, and put it on a little table in front of the sofa. I passed Reg his tea and took a slurp of mine. I looked around the tidy room. In one corner stood a dark brown cabinet with big glass doors. The shelves inside were crammed full of old stuff. Reg once said that the contents of that cabinet were priceless, but it all looked like a pile of junk if you asked me.

I took the lid off the cookie tin and pointed it toward him. He took three and sat back, resting two on his chest and dunking the other in his tea.

"So, Maxwell. How's things?" he said. This was Reg's way of trying to work out who I was.

"Not very good actually, Reg. I've had a very bad day," I said. "I got in trouble again. First, I told everyone about the TV crew coming to the Hundredth Anniversary Celebration tomorrow. Then I was messing about in PE, and I banged heads with Charlie Geek. He got a nosebleed and there was blood *everywhere* and he fainted, and the school thinks I did it on purpose. But I didn't! I really didn't. It was a complete accident."

Reg nodded as he listened.

"I see . . . I see . . . Got a big nose, has he?"

"Sorry?"

Reg picked up a cookie from his chest and dunked it in his tea. "This Charlie fellow."

"Um, no. Not particularly. Anyway . . . that doesn't matter. What matters is that I'm not allowed to go to the Hundredth Anniversary Celebration tomorrow. *The Jed and Baz TV Roadshow* is going to be there! They're recording at our school! And now . . . and now I've got to miss it."

I felt my eyes filling up as I bit my lip.

Reg nodded a few times as he finished his cookie. I watched him, waiting for him to say something as he picked the crumbs off his sweater with his fingertips. There was a long pause, and then: "Have I ever shown you my collection of mermaid scales?"

I sighed. I don't know why I expected Reg to have any words

of wisdom; he lived in his own world too much. I gave him a weak smile.

"Mermaid scales? No. No, Reg, you haven't."

He put his tea down and levered himself up.

"Ah, come with me, then, and I'll show you," he said, grinning as he headed toward the glass cabinet. I put my mug down and followed him. When he opened the cabinet doors, a whiff of dust and something gross filled my nostrils. It smelled like something was rotting in there. What looked like an old leather shoe was propped up against the side of the glass, and I suspected that that was probably the cause of the revolting stench. He moved an old globe to one side, took out a plastic tub, pried the lid off, and pointed it toward me.

"Here they are," he said in a whisper. "Mermaid scales . . ."

I peered inside. Lying at the bottom of the tub was a big pile of teardrop-shaped objects. I picked one out and held it up to the light. It was smooth and shiny and felt like plastic. I knew exactly what they were.

"Reg, these are guitar picks. You use them to strum a guitar. To pick the strings. They're not mermaid scales."

Reg frowned, then scurried his hand around in the tub.

"Guitar picks? But my grandfather never played the guitar. Why would he keep such things? Let me see . . ." His face scowled as he searched. "There must be some scales in here somewhere; where are they?" He began to shake the box around, and a couple of picks flew out and onto the floor.

"Don't worry, Reg," I said, picking them up and putting them back. "Let's find the mermaid scales another day, eh?"

He stared at the tub, looking confused.

"Hey, what's this thing?" I said, picking up the flat leather shoe. "This looks *really* cool."

Reg quickly put the lid back on the box of picks.

"Ah! You've found the dead pirate's shoe! Wonderful, wonderful."

"Dead pirate?!" I said, dropping it on the floor.

"Careful, Maxwell! That's precious, that is!" He bent down and picked it up, turning it over and over in amazement.

"Where did it come from?" I said, wiping my hands on my trousers.

"My grandfather traded his best boots for this old shoe when he was in the depths of the Amazon rain forest. Apparently, it belonged to a treacherous pirate who sailed the Pacific Ocean in the eighteenth century."

Reg chuckled to himself as he stared at the shrunken shoe.

"Because he'd given away his boots, he had to do the rest of his trip wearing this one shoe! He was such a character, my grandfather."

He put it back into the cupboard and picked up an oval-shaped piece of wood the size of his palm. It looked like a wooden egg and around the outside was a delicate, carved pattern. He held it up.

"What's that?" I asked.

Reg put his head to one side.

"It's a box," he said. "A music box."

I stared at the strange wooden egg. "A box? It doesn't look like a box. How do you open it?"

Reg didn't say anything.

"Can I have a look?" I said. He paused for a moment and then passed it to me. It was quite heavy and I needed two hands to hold it. I turned it around carefully and examined the surface, which was carved with tiny swirling patterns.

"There's no way of opening it," I said, looking at it closely. I gave it a little shake. I could hear something rattling. "What's inside?"

Reg frowned at the egg and rubbed his eyebrow.

"I can't . . . I can't remember," he said sadly. It was as though the answer were locked away in his brain but he'd lost the key.

"Let's not worry about it now, eh, Reg?" I said. I put the carved wooden egg back on the cabinet shelf, where it wobbled and then lay on its side, resting against a black felt hat.

I reached for the old globe that was wedged in a corner. It was so faded you could barely make out the outline of the countries, and there were tiny holes punctured here and there.

"What do all these holes mean?" I asked. Reg opened his mouth, but he just looked blank.

"I . . . I don't know . . ." he said. He looked embarrassed, so I quickly put the globe back and closed the cabinet doors.

"I know! Should we have another cookie?" I said, and Reg's face brightened.

"What a marvelous idea! Let's do that," he said, heading back to his armchair. He sat down and picked up another snickerdoodle.

"That's rotten about not being able to go to your big school party," he said. "You must have been looking forward to that for a long time."

He had been listening after all. I felt a knot in the middle of my stomach tighten. He was right; it was rotten and it wasn't fair.

"I can't believe they're not letting me go after *everything* I've done for them," I said, digging my nails into my palms.

"Well, it can't be helped," said Reg, brushing crumbs from his chin. "If the school has said you can't go, then that's it, I guess. Rules are rules."

I looked at Reg, and he frowned at me as a big smile spread across my face.

"Ah, but I don't do 'rules,' Reg," I said, raising my eyebrows and giving them a little wiggle. I took another cookie and sat back on the sofa. My heart raced as I thought of my plan.

"Maxwell Beckett is going to the ball, whether they like it or not," I said.

CHAPTER 8
BALL

Bex spent five hours getting ready. FIVE. Whenever I went to use the bathroom, she was in there, steam escaping from underneath the door as if she was concocting some strange experiment inside. I've never known her to take so long to get ready for anything. She came out with a towel wrapped around her, then disappeared into her bedroom for such a long time that Mum had to knock to check that she was okay. Bex let her in and closed the door, but I could still hear them through the wall. She was saying something about her dress not looking right and thinking everyone would laugh at her.

I'd never known Bex to be that bothered about her clothes before, unlike a lot of the other girls at school. I'd seen Claudia Bradwell in the playground boasting about her dress for weeks, showing everyone pictures on her phone while the other girls oohed and aahed over it and told her how amazing she'd look. Bex had gone shopping with Mum last Saturday. They were out all day, and when they came home Bex ran upstairs carrying a big silver bag, which she hid in her room. Dad and I hadn't seen what she'd picked, but whatever it was, she was clearly having second thoughts about it now.

I hung around in my bedroom, trying to hear what was going on, and eventually Bex's door opened and Mum came out with a fixed grin on her face.

"Ah, Maxwell. Look at your beautiful sister. She looks

amazing, doesn't she?" She held the door and Bex appeared wearing a pale yellow dress. Her hair was curled and piled on top of her head, and her face looked kind of orange. Her shoulders were rolled forward as if she were trying to fold up into herself.

"Wow, Bex," I said. "You look . . . you look a bit . . ." Bex narrowed her eyes at me.

"She looks beautiful. That's what you were going to say. Isn't it, Maxwell?" Mum said, fixing me with a glare.

"Well . . . actually, I was just going to say that—"

"Right!" interrupted Mum. "Shall we go and show your dad? Come on."

Mum put her arm around Bex's shoulder, but she shrugged her off. She stared at me, and I stared back at her, and then she turned to Mum.

"I'm getting changed," she said. She ran to her room and slammed the door. Mum glared at me.

"What did you do that for?" she said.

I couldn't believe it.

"What? I didn't do anything!" I said.

Mum rubbed at her face.

"It took me ages to convince her she looked lovely. Why do you *always* have to spoil everything, Maxwell? Why?"

I could see tears beginning to fill her eyes.

"B-but I didn't say anything!" I said. Mum turned away and went downstairs. A few minutes later, Bex appeared from her bedroom wearing her black skinny jeans and her favorite gray top with HISTORY AIN'T DEAD written on the front. On her feet she wore some scruffy sneakers. She'd wiped most of the makeup off her face and arranged her hair into a braid that she wore on one side. She looked more like my sister again. I gave her a smile, but she just gave me a blank look and went downstairs. I followed.

"Bex! There you are," said Dad nervously. He looked at what she was wearing. "Oh, aren't you going to the ball?"

"Yes, I'm going," said Bex, sniffing.

Dad nodded his head.

"I see . . . Okay . . . Well, that's great! You look . . . nice," Dad said. "Very dark."

Bex ignored him and stood facing the window with her shoulders hunched, waiting for her friend Maddy to arrive. Maddy's uncle had a posh car that he rented out for weddings, and he was going to drive them to school, even though it was just a few blocks away.

We all waited in silence. I went to say something, but Mum and Dad shot dagger-eyes at me, so I kept quiet. At seven o'clock, a long silver car pulled up outside, and we all followed Bex to the door. Maddy's uncle got out and opened a back door, and Maddy emerged from beneath a rustle of gold material. Her face dropped when she saw Bex.

"You're wearing . . . *jeans*?" she said.

Bex nodded.

"Yeah, a dress isn't my style," she said. She gave Maddy a twirl and a curtsy and they both giggled.

"You look great, Maddy," shouted Dad. "Very shiny!" Mum elbowed him in the side.

Maddy looked down at the gold fabric, and her teeth gritted

into a smile. I think she was a bit jealous that she hadn't been brave enough to wear jeans as well. Bex dived into the back of the car and Maddy followed, and they both giggled as they rolled around on the squishy leather seats. Maddy's uncle slammed the car door shut, and we waved them off and then went back inside. Dad put his hand on my shoulder.

"I have to say, Max, you're handling this whole situation so well. It must really hurt being the only one in the school not going tonight. And . . . well . . . you've been really grown-up about it all."

Mum sighed. "I'm sure Maxwell doesn't want to be reminded about what he's missing right now, Eddie."

Dad turned to face her. "Now what? I'm just saying how proud I am of him. Can't I tell my own son that?"

Mum folded her arms. "By reminding him that he's the only person not allowed to go? Yeah, that's great, that is . . . I'm sure that's made him really happy. Isn't that right, Maxwell?"

They both stared at me. Waiting for me to take a side.

When they realized I wouldn't, Dad started up again. "And you're blaming him for making Bex change her outfit. That's not right, you know. That's not right at all."

"I'm not *blaming* him!" shrieked Mum. I could tell it was about to escalate into a full-on shouting match, so I ran to the kitchen.

"See what you've done?" screamed Mum.

"What *I've* done? Blimey, Amanda. You really take the cake sometimes. How about what *you've* done for a change?" Dad yelled back.

Monster was snoring in his bed, so I sat down beside him and stroked his ears. He stirred and looked up at me briefly, then let out a long deep breath and closed his eyes as he smacked his lips together. As I stroked him, I tried to block out the arguing from the hallway.

"Why don't you just *leave*, Eddie? If you hate it here so much, why don't you just pack a bag and go?"

I held my breath. Dad said something quietly back to her, but I couldn't hear what it was. They were talking in whispers now, which was almost worse. At least I knew what they were saying when they shouted. I gave Monster a little kiss on the top of his head, then I got up and walked through the hallway and out the front door, slamming it hard behind me.

———

Jed and Baz were due to start recording at seven forty-five. By then everyone would be in the auditorium and too busy trying to get in front of the cameras to notice me slipping in the back.

I walked past Mrs. Banks's garden. The headless flamingo was still there, looking over the pond. Although it couldn't do much looking without a head. Reg's curtains were open, and I could see the TV flickering inside. For a moment I thought about going in and watching a wildlife documentary with him. He loved watching those. Mum and Dad would assume that was where I'd run off to anyway. It would have been the most sensible thing to do: to sit with Reg and watch TV. But when had I ever been sensible? And why watch TV on a screen when you've got the real thing in your school auditorium? Jed and Baz were right there, right now! It was too good to miss. And besides, I had no intention of being caught.

When I got to school, it was so busy it was easy to go unnoticed. There was a great big TV truck parked at the front, so I stood behind that and watched the TV crew walking around wearing headsets and carrying clipboards. A group of eighth graders emerged from a white stretch limousine. The girls were wearing long sparkly dresses that kept getting snagged around their feet, and the boys looked like they were wearing their dads' work suits. A woman with a TV camera on her shoulder began to film them, and the girls collapsed into giggles as the boys started pushing and shoving one another. The woman with the camera huffed, then went off to film someone else.

Mr. Howard and Ms. Huxley were at the door welcoming everyone inside. Mr. Howard was wearing a red bow tie, and every time someone gave him a ticket, he somehow made the bow tie do a little spin. It wasn't funny, it was cringey, but everyone laughed because they were in such a good mood. Ms. Huxley was laughing more than anyone, and he kept grinning at her. I bet they'll be engaged before long.

I obviously couldn't go through the main entrance because I'd be spotted straightaway, so I planned to go around to the back of the school and in through the PE changing rooms. The changing rooms have a door that leads out onto the playing fields, and the inside door comes out on a long corridor at the side of the auditorium. From there I could slip in at the back without being seen.

I waited until everyone had gone inside and there were just a couple of the TV people around by the truck. Spotlights were swirling around the inside of the auditorium, and my stomach flipped over knowing that Jed and Baz were backstage right now, probably getting their TV makeup put on. This was going to be *brilliant.* I dug my fists into my pockets, put my head down and then walked right across the playground. I was nearly around the corner when:

"Hey! Where you going?"

I glanced behind me. A man from the production crew wearing headphones was glaring at me.

I waved to him as if to say, *It's fine. I'm supposed to be here!*

"Can someone see what that kid's up to?" I heard him say, but then a woman with a clipboard distracted him.

As I arrived beside the auditorium, I could hear Mrs. Lloyd, the principal, talking into a microphone.

"Well, thank you, everyone, for coming . . . I just want to say a few words before Jed and Baz come onto the stage and we start recording . . ."

There was a huge scream inside the auditorium, and it took Mrs. Lloyd a while to calm everyone down. I ran around the outside. They'd probably given Jed and Baz the area behind the stage as a dressing room. It was crazy to think they were so close! They were probably the most famous TV presenters in the country right now! I got to the changing rooms, but when I tried the boys' door it was locked. The girls' was locked as well. Then I spotted the boiler room. It was out-of-bounds for all students *and* teachers, and the only person who had a key was Mr. Farrow, the caretaker. There was a little square sign screwed to the door that had an outline of someone getting electrocuted and underneath it read:

HIGH VOLTAGE

I wouldn't normally notice the door, but this evening there

was something different about it. The key was still in the lock. Mr. Farrow must have been so busy getting things ready that he'd accidentally left it behind. I took a quick look around, opened the door, and slipped the key into my pocket.

The door was very heavy, probably for fire protection, and when it shut behind me the room was plunged into darkness. I felt along the wall and found a light switch, and a bulb above my head flickered on. I took a look around. Along one wall were lots of fuse boxes and metal cupboards with black handles. There was a storage area with some stepladders, brooms, mops, and buckets, and beyond that was another door that opened onto the corridor beside the auditorium. I knew that this door also had a HIGH VOLTAGE sign on the other side, as I'd walked past it hundreds of times, going to and from lessons. I twisted the handle. It was locked, but when I tried the key from the outside door, it turned. I slowly opened it and peeked out. The corridor was empty, and a countdown was starting in the auditorium. Jed and Baz were going to be leaping onto the stage in exactly twenty seconds' time. My stomach fizzled. I quickly slipped out of the door and closed it behind me.

"Maxwell! What are you doing here?!"

I froze. I recognized the voice immediately.

"Mum and Dad are going to be so mad!"

I turned around and saw my sister at the end of the corridor in a dark corner. She was almost invisible in her black jeans and gray top. She looked really, really angry.

"You're going to be in *so* much trouble, Maxwell Beckett. You wait till I tell them," she said, walking up to me.

I shrugged.

"Don't care. I'm not missing Jed and Baz for *anything*," I said. "Bex? Are you all right?"

It looked like she'd been crying. My sister never cried, even when things got really bad at home. She scowled and quickly wiped at her cheeks. The countdown in the auditorium was coming to an end.

"Three, two, one!"

And then there was an almighty cheer as Jed and Baz walked out onto the stage. They were playing their theme tune! The crowd was going absolutely crazy, and I really wanted to go and see what was going on, but I couldn't leave my sister like this.

"What's happened?" I said.

She did a huge sniff.

"Claudia said . . . she said one of the TV people told the cameraman not to get me in any of the shots because I looked too weird."

I swallowed. That was pretty awful.

"And you believed her?" I said. "Really, Bex? Come on, there's no way that's true. Claudia Bradwell is just a waste of oxygen, and so is that brainless group that hangs around with her."

Bex smiled, wiping at her eyes again.

"Do you think so?" she said.

I nodded quickly and tried not to fidget too much. The sound from the auditorium was deafening now.

"I care what they think, you know?" she said. "I don't know why, but I do. *Everyone* takes notice of what Claudia says, and now everyone is laughing. Even Maddy! She was fine in the car, but when we got here, she just disappeared. It's like she's too embarrassed to be seen with me."

I shook my head and laughed.

"Maddy? She looks like she's had a fight with a candy wrapper!"

My sister smiled a little and wiped her nose.

"Sometimes . . . sometimes I think it would just be easier if I tried to be more like them, you know?" said Bex. "I could try and be friends with them and be a part of their group, and then they'd just leave me alone."

I huffed.

"Come on, Bex," I said. "Have you forgotten about the school carnival?"

My sister had been given a tough time by Claudia for years, but it had gotten much worse last summer. Bex won a big raffle prize at the school fete—a huge basket full of makeup and smelly bath stuff—and then, suddenly, Claudia was sniffing around her being all friendly. Claudia told her that she *was* allowed to be part of the group after all, but Bex saw straight through it. She shared the prize between Maddy and Mum and, after that, Claudia made sure that Bex's life at school was pretty hellish. There was one point where no one talked to my sister for three whole weeks; it was like she had turned invisible. Mum and Dad got involved then and spoke to the school, and after that things got a bit better. I didn't want to see her going back to being miserable like that again, no matter how much she annoyed me.

I could hear Jed and Baz firing T-shirts into the crowd now. They did that on all their TV programs. They had this cannon thing that shot them out into the air, and everyone tried to grab one, even though it was a pretty cheap top with their faces on the front.

I began to jiggle on the spot. I really, *really* wanted to get to the auditorium to try and win a T-shirt.

"What were you going to say, Maxwell? When I was wearing the dress? You said I looked a bit . . . and then Mum stopped you."

The noise from the auditorium was so loud now that I had to shout.

"I was going to say you looked a bit like a stranger. That's all. You didn't look like my sister!"

She blinked at me, dabbing at her nose with a tissue.

"I wasn't being rude. No matter what Mum thought. *This* is you," I said, pointing at her gray HISTORY AIN'T DEAD T-shirt. "It's a good thing you're not like Claudia and her witches. Not a *bad* thing!"

She wrinkled her nose and another small smile formed on her lips.

"They don't like you because you're a nerdy geek and you like history and you get your homework in on time, and that is *really* annoying . . ."

She opened her mouth to object.

"But! But . . . that's how your brain is wired. Just like Claudia's brain is wired to be evil."

Bex grinned.

"I hated that dress," she said. "I wanted to wear this, but I went along with it because it was making Mum happy. And she hasn't been happy for a while now, has she?"

I shook my head.

"Or Dad," I said. I stared down and scuffed the wooden floorboards with my toe.

"You really shouldn't be here, you know. You'll get into a ton of trouble if you're spotted," said Bex.

"I know. All I'm going to do is to sneak in the back, watch a little bit, then go home. I'm not doing any harm."

She nodded.

"Okay. Well, go on in, then, before you miss it." I grinned at her. She grinned back and then I ran off.

Little did I know, the next time I saw my sister, she would have no idea who I was.

CHAPTER 9
ELECTRICITY

Jed and Baz were amazing. AMAZING. They were so funny, and everyone was laughing and grinning and cheering for them. They do this thing on the show where you can get a really big prize just by winning a party game. One sixth grader got an Xbox for coming in first in a game of musical statues. It was wild! Normally I would have been up at the front trying to get them to pick me, but I had to keep out of the way of any TV cameras in case I was spotted. Being seen would have been an absolute disaster.

Jed shouted into the microphone that the next game was going to be Pin the Tail on the Donkey. They brought out a great big picture of a donkey, but it had Baz's goofy face on it, and everyone cracked up laughing.

"Guys! Are you ready to win more prizes?!" screamed Jed. Everyone roared "Yes!" back at him and put their arms up in the air, including me.

I spotted Charlie Geek by the side of the stage. He had something on his face, and at first I thought he was wearing some weird costume, but then I realized it was a great big bandage across his nose. He was jiggling around like he had a wasp in his pants, with his arm stretched up in the air.

"This is going to be a tough one, Jed," said Baz, looking out at the sea of hands. "How are we going to decide who has the chance to win . . ."

There was a drumroll. Jed and Baz put their arms around each other, then shouted, ". . . A TRIP TO FLORIDA!!!"

Everyone went crazy as Jed and Baz suddenly jumped down off the stage and walked straight into the crowd.

"Right, I'm going to go and pick our first contestant," said Baz. Everyone was screaming and waving their arms in his face, trying to get him to pick them. He turned around, and Charlie Geek was standing right in front of him.

"Nice nose-wear!" he said. I could see Charlie's eyes go all wide and he pulled his stupid duck face, which must have been quite difficult to do with all those bandages on. Baz did his goofy face back and patted him on the shoulder.

"You're the first contestant, my friend!" he said, and everyone cheered. Charlie bounced up and down like he was on an invisible pogo stick, and then he made his way to the steps by the side of the stage.

"How are you getting on, Jed?" shouted Baz across the auditorium. Jed was just a few yards from me. The kids around him were pushing and shoving each other, begging to be picked.

"I think I'm going to have to decide another way!" he shouted into the microphone. "It's time for Picky Pointer!"

The crowd jumped up and down and clapped as he began to spin around and around and around, faster and faster with his finger pointing outward. He did this on every show, and sometimes he went so fast he fell over. After a few turns he began to slow down.

"I think I'll choose . . . YOU!" he said. He stopped spinning and pointed his finger straight at me. I looked up. My arm was still in the air.

There was a general gasp from the audience as I stood there, my mouth dangling open.

"Come on now, don't be shy. You want to win a vacation, don't you?" said Jed. Behind him was a woman with a camera on her shoulder, and she was pointing it directly at me. I was going to be on TV! I opened my mouth to say something, when all of a sudden Mrs. Lloyd pushed her way through the crowd.

"No, no, no. Stop filming! Stop filming!" she said. "*He's* not supposed to be here." She stood in front of me with her hands on her hips. Jed looked at her, then back at me, and then he swiped his hand across his throat and the music cut out.

Mr. Howard appeared beside him. His bow tie wasn't spinning anymore.

"Maxwell! Get yourself home," he said through gritted teeth. "Don't make a scene." The camerawoman turned toward him. She was still filming. The auditorium was silent now and all you could hear was the hum of the lights.

I stayed exactly where I was and folded my arms.

"You can't make me," I said. Jed snorted and I grinned at him, but he just scowled back.

Mrs. Lloyd stepped toward me.

"Maxwell Beckett, you need to leave the auditorium immediately," she said under her breath. The camera moved around to film her, but she tried to move out of the way.

"I'M NOT GOING ANYWHERE!" I bellowed.

A woman with a clipboard came over to Jed.

"I think we need to take a few minutes to sort this out, okay,

Jed?" she said to him. He rolled his eyes and gave a massive huff. Baz appeared beside him.

"What's going on? Are we doing this thing or not? Who's this dude?" he said, nodding toward me and looking at me like I was a piece of dirt on the floor.

I could feel my eyes stinging as everyone stared. Behind the crowd I could see Charlie standing on the stage beside the donkey picture. He was shaking his head at me.

"Maxwell, you're making a spectacle of yourself. Now, be a sensible boy and go home," Mrs. Lloyd said sternly. Mr. Howard looked at me sadly. He was about to say something to Mrs. Lloyd when Jed pushed by him.

"Hey, man," he said. "I don't know what you've done, but you're kinda ruining this for me and Baz here."

I stared back at him. I couldn't believe it. Jed hated me! Baz appeared beside him.

"Jed's right," he said. "It's time for you to get outta here, don't cha think?"

I stared at them as Jed put his hand on Baz's shoulder. They both glared back at me.

"You're . . . you're rubbish anyway!" I shouted. There was a huge gasp, and then I turned and pushed my way through the crowd and out of the auditorium.

"Maxwell. Wait!" called Mr. Howard, but I was gone. I was so outta there.

"Okay, guys, let's get this party started!" screamed Baz into his microphone, and the crowd gave a unanimous whoop. I got back to the corridor and dived into the HIGH VOLTAGE boiler room, locking the door behind me. Someone started pounding on it from the other side.

"Maxwell, you know you're not allowed in there! Now, open the door and let's have a chat, shall we?" It was Mr. Howard.

I stared around the little room, my eyes wet with tears. He banged again.

"Come on, Maxwell. I'm sure we can have a word with Mrs. Lloyd," he said. "I'll see if she will let you stay. How about that?"

"Go away!" I shouted. There was no way I'd go back in that auditorium, even if she said yes.

I made my way past the mops and brushes toward the fuse boxes and electric switches. I looked up. I knew exactly what I was looking for and I spotted it straightaway—a bright red switch with one word printed underneath it: MAIN.

I upturned a metal bucket, stood on top, and then reached up and held the big switch between my thumb and forefinger.

"Everything's gone wrong . . ." I whispered, and then, click, I flicked the switch. The music from the auditorium instantly died, along with the lightbulb above my head. I got down off the bucket and felt my way along the wall until I got to the door that led outside. I went out and locked it behind me, putting the key into my pocket. And then I ran. I ran as fast as I could from the worst day of my life.

CHAPTER 10
EGG

Hundreds of students were spilling out onto the playground now that the school was in darkness. Some were holding on to each other and using the flashlights on their cell phones. The teachers guided everyone out, trying to keep people calm. I stood in the shadows beside the back of the auditorium and watched.

"Are Jed and Baz . . . are they going to stay and finish the show?" said a sixth grader. My PE teacher, Mrs. Allen, put her hand on her shoulder.

"We're trying to get the power back on, but if we can't . . . well, I don't know what will happen, I'm afraid," she said.

I moved behind a tree near the TV truck. One of the crew was inside the back of the truck shouting at someone about a generator and the fact that it hadn't been repaired. A posh black car was parked behind the truck, and I could just make out Jed and Baz in the back. They were both wearing baseball caps and talking on their cell phones. The car slowly pulled away.

"Look! It's Jed and Baz!" a boy cried out. "They're leaving!"

There was a general wail from the crowd, and a few people started to cry. Mrs. Lloyd came out of the auditorium and clapped her hands together.

"Listen up, please, everyone! Listen up!" Everyone hushed. "In light of the current situation with the power, I'm afraid to say . . . tonight's ball has been canceled . . ."

The sound of wailing echoed around the playground.

"B-b-but why?" said a sixth grader.

"They can't record a TV show without any power, can they?" replied a tenth grader. The wailing got louder, and Mrs. Lloyd had to shout over it.

"A text message has been sent out to all your grown-ups to come and collect you as soon as possible," she said. Her voice was shaking a bit.

Charlie Geek appeared from the door. "Why did the power go off in the first place, miss? Can't it be fixed? Don't the TV people have a generator?"

Mrs. Lloyd shook her head.

"I'm afraid not, Charlie. Apparently there's a problem with their generator, and the main switch in the boiler room has been turned off. Whoever did it has deliberately locked the room behind them, and there is no spare key. Mr. Farrow is trying to track down a locksmith, but it's all going to be too late."

Marcus appeared beside Mrs. Lloyd, his face lit up by his phone.

"It was Maxwell Beckett who did it. Wasn't it?" he said. "He was in the auditorium and then he legged it and *then* the electricity went off. Don't tell me it was a coincidence. It was him! Maxwell Beckett has ruined *everything!*"

The wailing stopped now and the crowd began to mumble and growl. Mrs. Lloyd tried to calm them all down. I swallowed and felt a tight lump in my throat.

"That's enough, everyone!" said Mr. Howard. "I said, that's

enough! We don't know what has happened yet, so nobody should be jumping to any conclusions. And that means you, too, Marcus."

I was pleased that my homeroom teacher was trying to stick up for me, but it wasn't helping.

"He should be expelled, sir!" shouted Adel from my class. "Especially after what he did to Charlie's nose."

"Yes! No one likes him anyway. It's not like he'd be missed," said a girl who I think was in the seventh grade. I didn't even know who she was. I couldn't believe it. Everybody really did hate me.

"OUT WITH MAXWELL! OUT WITH MAXWELL!" someone started to chant, and before long everyone began to join in. It reminded me of an old black-and-white film set in medieval times that Dad used to watch. A stranger moved to a village, and there was a big angry mob that wanted to get rid of him. One day they all got together and chased him out of town. I almost expected to see one of my schoolmates raise a burning stake above their head as they searched for me on the school grounds.

The chanting grew louder and louder, and while the teachers tried to calm everyone down, I ran off before I was spotted.

———

I didn't want to go home. Mum and Dad might have stopped arguing by now, but as soon as they found out what had happened at school, it would all start again. No. I would go to the place where I felt most safe. Reg's.

I burst in through his kitchen door.

"Reg? It's me. Can I . . . can I stay here for a bit?"

Reg appeared in the living room doorway, a flustered look on his face.

"What? Who are you?" he said, holding on to the doorframe.

"It's me, Reg. Maxwell. You know who I am! I see you nearly every day. You're just going to have to trust me on that. I can't . . . I can't explain it all again right now . . ."

I think he could tell I'd been crying. He stared at me for a bit and then walked into the kitchen.

"Sit yourself down, young Maxwell. I'll get us a drink and some cookies. How about that?"

I breathed out with relief.

"Thanks, Reg. That would be lovely," I said. I went into the living room and slumped onto the sofa. I was exhausted. I thought of all the chaos I'd left behind at school. There must have been hundreds of angry parents arriving now, demanding to know who was to blame for their child being so upset.

Reg appeared with the cookies and two glasses of orange juice on a tray. He put them down on the little table and took the lid off the tin, pointing it toward me.

"Now. Tell me all about yourself, and let's see if you can jog a few memories."

I took a ginger cookie from the tin.

"I'm Maxwell Beckett. I'm twelve years old and . . . everybody hates me," I said.

Reg took a sip of his orange juice.

"Well, that's quite a big thing to say, young Maxwell. Why would everyone hate you?"

I began to eat the cookie, taking tiny bites around the edge.

My throat still had a huge lump in it and I didn't really want the cookie, but concentrating on each nibble calmed me down.

"They hate me because I'm . . . me," I said.

"But they can't hate you for just being you," he said. He began eating his cookie in the same way, taking tiny bites around the outside in an ever-decreasing circle.

"Everybody hates me because . . . because I'm a loser and I'm always getting into trouble. Everything I do goes wrong. *Everything*."

I could feel Reg staring at me as I carried on.

"My best friend hates me . . . In fact, everyone in my school hates me . . . even the teachers."

Reg put his head to one side.

"And what about your family? I bet they don't dislike you."

I turned and faced him, swallowing back the tears.

"My parents are too busy hating each other . . . but . . . but they don't get on because of me. It's all my fault. If I didn't get into so much trouble, then they wouldn't argue so much and maybe they'd actually like each other."

Reg took the cookie out of his mouth.

"Well, I don't hate you, Maxwell. You did that marvelous drawing of me, for a start, didn't you?" He pointed to the framed picture on his mantelpiece, the one I'd drawn for the school competition. He'd actually remembered something for a change. I looked at the picture that I'd drawn of Reg, which was one of the few things I was truly proud of. Although, this evening it didn't look as good; the nose was wonky and the eyes weren't level.

"That picture is rubbish. You should just throw it away," I said.

Reg sighed.

"It sounds to me, young Maxwell, like you've just had a particularly bad day. We all have them. I've had plenty in my time, I can tell you."

His pale gray eyes stared off toward the wall for a moment, and then he returned to me.

"However, because you've had a bad day today doesn't always mean that tomorrow will be the same, or the day after that or the day after that."

He started eating his cookie again.

"But you don't understand," I said. "I make everybody's lives worse. My best friend, Charlie Geek, wouldn't have hurt his nose if it wasn't for me, the TV show wouldn't have been canceled . . . my parents wouldn't argue . . . I'm a disaster. After what I've done, there is no way anyone is going to speak to me ever again. *Anyone.* Everyone hates me so much."

I shut my eyes and put my head in my hands. The room was quiet for a moment, and then I heard Reg give a big sigh.

"Have I ever shown you the dodo's feather?"

I wiped my face with my hands and looked up at him. Reg brushed cookie crumbs from his sweater.

"Dodo's feather?" I asked.

He smiled.

"Yes! You know. That silly bird that became extinct? Would you fetch it for me? It's in the cabinet."

Reg reached into the tin for cookie number three.

"Look for a cardboard box marked *DODO.*"

I sighed. This was all I needed: having to poke around his creepy cabinet. I stood up and walked to the glass doors and peered inside. The pirate's shoe was still propped against one side, and the plastic tub full of what Reg thought were mermaid scales was at the back. The old, dark globe speckled with holes was balanced on the shelf next to a black hat and the large, wooden, egg-shaped music box that didn't open.

I moved a few things around, trying to find the dodo feather among all the junk. There was a small cardboard box at the back, and as I reached for it I knocked the globe with my elbow. It crashed to the floor along with the black hat, the shoe, the box of mermaid scales, and the carved wooden egg.

"Maxwell! What are you doing? Be careful!" said Reg, from his armchair.

"See what I told you?!" I whined. "I can't do *anything* right."

I looked down and huffed. The guitar picks had come out of their box and were everywhere.

"Make sure you put everything back properly, won't you, Maxwell?" called Reg.

I sighed, then got down on my hands and knees and began to pick up all the pieces of plastic and put them back into the little tub. There were hundreds of them, so it took ages. After I'd finished, I picked up the globe and sat back on my heels.

"Do you know? Sometimes I think everyone would be better off if I'd never existed in the first place," I muttered. I turned the globe over in my hands as I stared at the faded countries. I sighed and stood up and wedged the globe on a shelf between a dusty old umbrella and a dirty-looking vase.

I picked up the black hat and put that back on the shelf, then lifted the shoe using my fingertips. I quickly threw it on the shelf, checking that Reg wasn't watching. The egg had rolled toward the back of the sofa. I went over and picked it up.

"Why can I not do *anything* right?" I said, turning the egg over in my hands. There was a little wooden knob on the top. I twisted it a couple of times to the right. It made a tiny *ticker-ticker-ticker* noise, like an old watch being wound.

"What was that, Maxwell?" said Reg from his chair.

"It's fine," I said. "I'm just . . . I'm just picking things up and putting them away like you asked me to."

I held the egg in the palm of my hand and traced some of the carvings with my finger.

"There's no point in me really, is there?" I said, very quietly. "I just wish . . . I wish I'd never been born."

I gave the egg a shake. There were three strained *plink, plonk, plank* sounds and then it stopped. The noises reminded me of an old jewelry box that Bex used to have when she was little. You opened the top, and a plastic ballerina sprang up and twirled around as it played "Twinkle, Twinkle, Little Star."

I stared at the egg and took a deep breath, and then I stood up and placed it back on the shelf next to the hat and closed the cabinet door. I remembered I was supposed to be trying to find the dodo box.

"I'm not really in the mood to look at the feather right now, Reg. Is that okay?" I said, but when I turned around, Reg was sound asleep, his head tipped back and his mouth wide open. His nose was making a whistling sound as he breathed.

"Oh, well, that's just great," I said.

I looked around the room, then sighed again. There wasn't really anything else I could do. I'd have to go home and own up to what had happened at school. Mrs. Lloyd would have rung my mum and dad by now, so there was no doubt about it.

I was in very big trouble indeed.

CHAPTER 11
GATE

I'd have to keep to the shadows on my way home. There would be a lot of parents driving past soon, picking up their crying children from the ball. I walked down Reg's pathway and looked left and right, but for now the road was deserted.

I turned past Mrs. Banks's house. Although it was dark, I could still make out the shape of the plastic flamingo watching over the pond.

I stopped.

Something had changed.

The flamingo had a head.

It hadn't had a head when I'd walked past it on the way to the ball. It had definitely been a headless flamingo.

I squinted into Mrs. Banks's living room. Her blinds were gaping a little, and I could see the silhouette of her sitting on the sofa. I guess she'd finally gotten around to buying a new flamingo. I stared at the plastic flamingo, and its black eye stared back at me. For a second I thought about throwing another brick at it, but I figured I was in enough trouble as it was.

I carried on walking, and every now and then I checked behind me for cars, but the road was deserted. There should have been hundreds of them by now, ferrying upset kids home from the ball. Where was everybody? Something didn't feel right. I just wanted to hurry up and get home, so I started to jog.

The first thing I planned to do when I got in was to head to the kitchen and give Monster a big hug. That would help me deal with facing Mum and Dad. Monster always made me feel better. I smiled to myself, but when I got to the house, my face dropped.

Something was wrong.

At the end of our path we had two columns of bricks, and in between them was a black iron gate.

The only trouble was . . . we didn't have a gate.

We *used* to have a gate, but I'd broken it about five years ago. I liked swinging on it as it made a funny creaking noise, even though Mum told me not to. Eventually the hinges buckled and the gate fell off.

I walked up to it and pushed it gently with my foot. It gave a low, growling squeak, just like our old one. In fact, this gate looked identical to the one we used to have. Mum and Dad were useless at mending things, and there was no way they'd have paid someone else to fix it. Where had it come from? The wind picked up, and I heard a scratchy noise coming from behind me. When I turned around, it was just a few leaves scattering along the dark, empty road.

I looked at my house. The lights were off and Mum's car and Dad's van were missing from the driveway. They hadn't said anything about going out. Maybe they were at the school picking up Bex? Or looking for me? But then surely they would have gone straight to Reg's house if they were worried about where I was. They knew I always went there.

"What's going on?" I whispered.

I walked up to the front door and knocked, as I didn't have my key.

Nothing.

I pressed the doorbell, even though I knew the battery had run out months ago.

PRRRIINNNGGGGG!

I jumped as it let out an urgent ring.

My heart pounded as the sound echoed through the house, and then there was silence. They must have just replaced the batteries and forgotten to mention it. It wasn't a big deal. I pressed the doorbell again and listened as the *PRRRIINNNGGGGG* blasted through the house again. No one came to answer.

I stood there for a moment, wondering what to do, and then I remembered we had a key hidden around the back in case any of us were locked out. There were two plant pots on either side of our back door, and Mum had hidden a spare key under the one on the left, but when I got there, the pots were gone. I stared at the space where they used to stand.

"Where are they?" I said out loud. Maybe Dad had moved them?

I tried the handle on the back door, but it was locked. I took a couple of steps back.

"Hold on . . . hold on . . ." I said to myself. "Keep it together. There must be a reasonable expla— WHOA!"

Suddenly an enormous black-and-white cat emerged through the kitchen-door cat flap. It blinked at me for a moment, then trotted off into the garden.

"B-but . . . we haven't got a cat!" I whispered. And the cat flap was always locked because Monster had a habit of poking his head through the hole and getting stuck.

I watched the cat sniff at a bush and then disappear into the darkness.

I felt dizzy and a bit sick. My heart was pounding madly. I spotted some plant pots near our patio door, and I ran over and quickly rolled each one out of the way to see if there was a key hidden underneath.

Nothing.

I tried the patio door.

Locked.

My head was spinning, and my legs began to shake. I knelt down onto the cold paving slabs, trying to work out what was happening. And then I pressed my forehead against the glass of the patio door and looked inside my house.

"No, no, no, no . . ." I said. "This cannot be real . . . This *cannot* be happening."

CHAPTER 12

KITCHEN

I stared in at our kitchen. Although it wasn't our kitchen anymore. The cupboards were the same, and the stove and the sink, but everything else was different. There was a circular table in one corner with a vase of flowers in the middle. Our table was oblong and wooden, and we certainly didn't have flowers in our house. Along the wall was a pine dresser with lots of blue-and-white dishes propped up on the shelves. It was all neat and tidy-looking. I leaned back from the glass and saw my reflection. My mouth opened and my lips mouthed one word:

"Monster . . ."

I quickly looked back into the kitchen, circling my eyes with my hands. The trash can was in the same place as ours, but it was black, not silver. And there was something missing next to it. Monster's bed.

"Monster? Are you in there?" I said, tapping on the glass. I tried to look to the left to see if I could spot his tail wagging behind the kitchen cabinets. I scanned around for his water and dinner bowls, but there was no sign of them, either.

Suddenly the kitchen light turned on, and I blinked as it dazzled my eyes. A strange man walked in and put a jacket over the back of a chair. He turned toward the patio door and jumped when he spotted me staring in through the glass. He rushed to the patio door, unlocked it, and yanked it open.

"What on earth do you think you're doing?!" he demanded.

"I'm . . . um . . . I was looking for someone."

He looked livid.

"WHO?" he bellowed.

I opened my mouth and closed it again. I was too frightened to say because I was worried about what his answer would be.

"Were you trying to break in?" he said. "Anyone else with you?" He looked over my head into the dark garden. I got up from the ground.

"I'm not trying to break in. Honestly! I was looking for the Becketts. Mr. and Mrs. Beckett? Amanda and Eddie? And a girl called Bex? They live here. And a dog. A beagle called Monster? Is he in there?"

The man suddenly seemed to understand what I was saying, and his shoulders dropped a little. I felt my own do the same.

"Oh, the Becketts! Yes, yes, I know who you mean . . ."

I sighed with relief. It was all fine. This had just been some kind of weird mix-up.

I smiled at him. "Could you get them for me, please?"

I moved to go inside, but the man blocked my way.

"Whoa, steady on a minute. You're not coming in," he said, folding his arms and glaring at me. "The Becketts moved out over a year ago. I bought this house after they got divorced. I'm not sure where they live now, but it certainly isn't here."

"Divorced . . . ?"

The man cocked his head to one side and stared at me.

"Hang on a minute . . . Are you *sure* you're not a burglar?"

My ears were ringing. Divorced? Moved out? What was going on? I took a few steps backward.

"Now get out of my garden and away from my property before I call the police. Do you hear me?"

I stared back at the strange man standing in the kitchen that wasn't my kitchen anymore.

And then I ran.

CHAPTER 13
RUNNING

I sprinted down the road. My head was buzzing as if the doorbell was still ringing in my ears.

What was happening? Where were Mum, Dad, Bex, and Monster? Had they had enough of me and moved away, all within the time I'd been at school? Surely that was impossible. But our furniture was gone. How could a strange man have moved in with his stuff in the time I was out? And besides, the man had said Mum and Dad were divorced, and that *definitely* hadn't happened.

I ran by Mrs. Banks's house, and on past Reg's toward Charlie Geek's road. Charlie was going to be really angry with me for ruining the whole TV recording, especially when he'd been about to get the chance to win an amazing vacation, but I didn't have anywhere else to try. I got to the end of the road, turned left, and then crossed over to Charlie's street. The roads were still deserted. I didn't see one car.

It was late now, and I was getting cold. I put my hands under my armpits and gave myself a sort-of-hug as I arrived at Charlie's house. He lived with his mum in a duplex, which is one house split into two. They lived in the bottom half and used the front door, and the people upstairs had a door around the side. I walked up to the front door and stood with my finger hovering over the doorbell. There was a light on, so it looked like they were home. I took a deep breath, then pushed the bell. A few seconds later the door opened, and Charlie's mum was standing there. I breathed a sigh of relief.

"Mrs. Geek! It's you! Brilliant. Is Charlie there?"

She frowned at me, and so I gave her my brightest smile, but I don't think it came out very well.

"I think you've got the wrong house," she said. "Who are you looking for again? Mrs. Geek, did you say?"

Of course! I was so used to calling my friend Charlie Geek that I almost thought of it as being his real name. I smiled at her. She must have been joking with me.

"I mean Kapoor. Hello, Mrs. Kapoor." I gave her another smile, but she was still frowning. "Is Charlie in?"

She looked me up and down.

"Wait there," she said, and went inside.

I pushed the door a little and peeked into their hallway. In one corner was their tall wicker basket that was supposed to hold long old-fashioned umbrellas but actually contained two lightsabers, a badminton racket, and a long pink spade. Next to the basket were Charlie's school shoes and backpack. I relaxed a little. Everything looked the same.

I smiled as I breathed in the delicious scent of their dinner, but my face dropped when Charlie appeared.

"Ch-Charlie?" I said. The boy standing in front of me was Charlie, but he looked so . . . different. His hair was short and shaved around the sides, and the top was all spiky like he'd put wax or gel in it. His nose looked fine, too. The bandage that he'd been wearing at the ball was gone.

"Yes?" he said, glaring at me.

"Hi! Wow, your nose looks better. Did I say how sorry I was about that? Well . . . I am. I'm *really* sorry. But I see you've got the bandage thingy off already, so I'm guessing there's not much damage or anything."

I nodded at him, smiling. He frowned and stroked the top of his nose, then looked back at me blankly. I cleared my throat.

"And the thing with the electricity at the school tonight, the Hundredth Anniversary Celebration? Well, that was just a whole other misunderstanding . . ." I did a little cough. "Your hair looks good, by the way. Did you get it cut?"

Charlie Geek put his hand to his hair and frowned.

"Hang on," he said. "Who are you?"

My legs began to tremble. I reached up and held on to the wall.

"Don't mess with me, Charlie," I said, doing a weak laugh. "It's me! Maxwell. Maxwell Beckett. Your best friend? Well, we were best friends until I hurt your nose. Which was an accident, obviously."

Charlie stared at the floor for a moment, and then he looked back up at me. His nose scrunched up like it does when he gets angry, and then he laughed. It was a weird laugh, though, kind of manic.

"Ha! Oh yeah, I get it. This is one of Marcus's pranks, isn't it? Ha! He's a funny one, isn't he? Ha! Well, you tell him I'll get him back tomorrow. Okay?"

I took a step forward and opened my mouth to say something, but— BANG! The door slammed in my face.

My stomach plummeted. Charlie Geek didn't know who I was! He really didn't have a clue. And his nose was absolutely fine—there was no sign that it had been hurt at all. I slowly walked down the path and turned left.

I was scared.

Something had gone wrong here.

Something had gone very wrong indeed.

CHAPTER 14
SOFA

There was only one place left I could go. Reg's bungalow.

Reg's kitchen light was on, and I knocked on the door. I'd usually walk straight in, but this time I waited for him to answer. When he opened the door, I got the reaction I was expecting.

"Can I help you?" he said, a puzzled look on his face. But then Reg always looked like that.

"It's me. Maxwell. Maxwell Beckett. Do you remember?"

He smiled but shook his head.

"I come and visit you most days and we sit in your living room and drink tea and eat cookies. We're . . . we're friends."

Reg studied me for a moment.

"Tea and cookies, you say? Well, that certainly sounds like a friend I'd have," he said, smiling. "And if you say you're Maxwell Beckett, then that's who you must be."

I smiled back at him.

"I . . . I'm sorry to knock so late. But . . . I wondered if I could come in?"

The wind got a little stronger, and Reg pulled his cardigan tighter around him, then opened the door a little wider.

"How about a hot chocolate?" he said. "I'll put the kettle on."

———

As he stirred the hot chocolate, I tried to explain how confused I was. He listened quietly as he poured the rest of the water from the kettle into an old blue hot-water bottle. He was clearly getting ready for bed.

"Everything looks different, you say?" he said.

"Yes. I don't understand it. My family . . . they're . . . they're not in our house anymore. There's a strange man living there with all his stuff. And . . . and Mrs. Banks's flamingo has got a head again . . ."

I picked up my mug, and we made our way to the living room.

"And Charlie . . . well, Charlie Geek doesn't even know who I am! And my dog, Monster. I . . . I don't know where he is, and I'm worried something might have happened to him."

Reg's eyes widened.

"Well, that really is a predicament, isn't it? What to do, though, eh? What to do."

I liked Reg, but he didn't fill me with much confidence. He sat back in his armchair and his soft gray eyes focused on me.

"And everything has been fine up to this point?" he said, hugging the hot-water bottle. "No sign of anything strange going on beforehand?"

"No. Although I have had a really bad week. And I mean *really* bad. I got into some big trouble at school. I accidentally head-butted my best friend, and . . . and I ruined the school's big Hundredth Anniversary Celebration when the TV crew was there. It was called off, all because of me." I sipped my hot chocolate. "Everybody hates me."

Reg's eyes were drooping.

"And what was the last thing you remember? Before everything changed?"

I took another sly look to my left. Reg's cabinet of curiosities was still there.

"Well, I ran away from the ball after I'd ruined everything. I didn't want to go home because I knew Mum and Dad would be arguing, so I came here."

Reg yawned.

"I see, I see," he said, rubbing at his eyes. "Well, I think what we should do is this. I think you should go home and get some sleep, and tomorrow we'll see if we can come up with a plan. Okay?"

I opened my mouth to remind him that I didn't have a home, but I closed it again.

"Okay, Reg. You head off to bed. I'll let myself out."

"Right you are," said Reg. He yawned again and then levered himself out of his armchair and shuffled toward the door that led to the hallway and his bedroom.

"Night, night, Maxwell Beckett," he said, and he closed the door behind him.

I looked at the sofa I was sitting on. I was going to have to sleep here. I wanted to be home, in my own bed, but there wasn't anything I could do about it. This was the only place I could stay.

I drank the rest of my hot chocolate, then put the empty mug on the coffee table. There was a gray woolly blanket on the back of his armchair, and I took that and arranged it over my legs the best I could. I plumped up a red cushion for a pillow and settled down as I waited for sleep to come. Reg was right. This would probably seem much better in the morning. There must be a reasonable explanation for what was happening. It was probably a big, elaborate hoax, planned between my parents and the school to teach me some kind of lesson. Yes, that's what it must be! Well, if that was what it was, then I'd show them. I wasn't going to give them the satisfaction of being upset or anxious or scared any longer. If they thought they could fool me, then they had another think coming.

CHAPTER 15
MORNING

I woke to the sound of shouting.

"Who are you?! And what are you doing on my sofa?"

Reg was standing by the sofa, holding his hot-water bottle up like it was some kind of weapon. I sat up.

"It's me, Reg! Maxwell! You let me sleep here last night. Remember? I came to see you because . . . because I was having a bad day. You said I could stay."

It felt bad lying, but I had to say something.

"Did I?" said Reg, putting the hot-water bottle down. He looked sad. "I don't remember that at all. I don't have the best memory, you see. It's a bit of a problem."

I rubbed the sleep out of my eyes.

"It's okay, Reg. I know all about it."

Reg looked embarrassed, so I tried to change the subject.

"This sofa is quite comfy, you know," I said, doing a little bounce. "I had a lovely sleep last night. Thank you!"

Reg smiled and nodded.

"That's good, that's good. Well, I'll go and see what I've got for breakfast, shall I?" He wandered off to the kitchen. My stomach churned a bit when I thought about home. There was no Mum and Dad, no Bex, and no Monster, but I still thought the most likely explanation was some kind of trick. They were obviously trying to teach me a lesson for all the bad stuff I'd done. The school was probably involved, too. I bet the evil Mrs. Lloyd was behind it!

"Toast all right for you, Maxwell?" called Reg from the kitchen. I hadn't eaten anything since yesterday afternoon and I was starving.

"Yes, please, Reg," I called back. I heard him switch the radio on.

Breakfast in bed! This wasn't so bad. I never got breakfast in bed at home. I stretched my arms and put them behind my head as I lay back and looked around Reg's living room.

Everything looked exactly the same. The beige curtains still hung at the window that looked out to the front garden. The old clock hanging on the wall by the door to the hallway was still ticking away. In the corner was the old curiosity cabinet, stuffed full of the usual junk. But over the fireplace, something was missing.

I stared at the empty space, and my stomach began to twist as though it was turning itself into a knot.

I pushed my blanket off and got up.

Reg was standing by the toaster when I went into the kitchen.

"Reg? Where is my picture?" I said.

The toaster popped, and he put a slice on each plate.

"Picture?" he said. "What picture would that be?"

I took a step closer toward him.

"The drawing I did of you. Do you know where it is? Mum had it framed. It was behind glass, and you had it on your mantelpiece in there. Right there in the living room," I said, jabbing my finger toward the room.

He stared at me blankly. I could feel my heart begin to pound. This was just making everything scary again.

"A drawing? No. No, I can't say I have any memory of that . . ."

He began to butter the toast, but I gripped his arm.

"But you must remember! Please, Reg. It's really important. I drew a picture of you. There was a big competition. You had to draw something that made you proud of your town, and I drew you! And I won! The school . . . the school got a lot of money and did lots of renovations. Reg? Please? You must know what I'm talking about!"

Reg was pressed against the kitchen counter as I held on to him. His worried look was back again—the one he did when he couldn't remember something.

"I'm so sorry, Maxwell, but I don't know about any picture."

I let go of his arm and ran into the living room and searched everywhere: behind cushions, under the sofa, behind the television. I opened the cabinet and started pulling everything out. Reg appeared, waving his arms.

"Oh no, no, no! My things . . . my things! Stop it! Stop what you're doing right now!"

Reg looked horrified.

"You can't do that with all my things, you can't!" he said. I stopped and looked down. The carpet was covered: the shriveled leather shoe, the dark globe, piles of old dusty books, and flimsy cardboard boxes. The carved wooden egg was in pieces. It was all just a pile of junk.

"But where is it?" I said. "Where is my picture?"

Reg looked at me blankly and shook his head.

"I'm sorry, Maxwell. I don't know," he said.

I grabbed my sweater from the sofa and put my shoes on.

"But where are you going?" said Reg, confused. "What about your toast?"

"I need to go and check something," I said, and I turned and ran out of the side door into the crisp autumn air.

There was only one way I would know what was going on and whether all this strangeness was just my family trying to teach me a lesson. And this time I knew exactly where to go.

My school.

CHAPTER 16
INVESTIGATION

I felt sick as I thought about the missing picture and everything else that had changed. If I could work out an explanation for each thing, then I knew I'd feel better. As I walked to school, I thought about it.

Number one: the new flamingo in Mrs. Banks's garden.

Although it was surprising that she'd swapped the headless one for a new one while I was at the Hundredth Anniversary Celebration, it was not exactly impossible. So that's what must have happened: Mrs. Banks had changed the flamingos during the evening. She wasn't part of any plan with my parents and the school to teach me a lesson. The new flamingo was just a coincidence.

Number two: our garden gate.

The garden gate looked exactly like the one I'd broken years ago. Dad must have replaced the buckled hinges and fixed it back onto the brick post. Dad was always pottering around outside, and I never usually noticed what he did in the garden, so why would I have seen this? He probably mended it weeks ago!

Number three: no sign of Mum, Dad, Bex, or Monster. No key under the plant pot. All our furniture gone. A strange man in our house. A cat.

This was harder to work out. The only explanation must be that Mum and Dad were so fed up with me they decided to teach me a lesson. The man in the house was probably a friend of Dad's and in on the joke. They'd moved the key, shuffled our furniture into another room, put some "fake" furniture in its place, and the scene was set. I bet my family was keeping Monster out of sight and giggling behind the kitchen door while my shocked face stared in through the patio door. The cat? Well, that was probably borrowed from someone up the road. There were loads of cats on our street, and we already had a cat flap, so that wasn't exactly hard.

Number four: Charlie Geek not knowing who I was and looking very different.

If number three was correct, then this was easy to explain. Mum and Dad must have told Charlie and his mum what they were planning and asked them to act like they didn't know me. He hated me! Of course he'd go along with it! He'd probably got his hair cut for the Hundredth Anniversary Celebration and I hadn't noticed. And he must have taken the bandage off when he'd gotten home, and the swelling on his nose must have gone down really, really quickly.

Number five: the missing portrait of Reg.

Reg is an elderly man who suffers from memory loss. He doesn't know who I am from one day to the next, so it was highly likely that he'd just moved the picture somewhere else and completely forgotten about it. Simple.

I smiled to myself. I felt a whole lot better already. My family would NEVER be able to put one over on me.

I reached the end of the road, turned right, and crossed over toward the school. It was Sunday, and I'd only seen three cars on my way there. I passed the two wide-trunked trees that stood by the front of the school. They looked exactly as they always did, standing on a patch of grass in front of the black gates where the

TV truck had been parked. I kicked at a pile of orange leaves, and they scattered onto the pavement, and then I looked up.

My arms felt heavy. It was as if all my insides were suddenly plummeting toward the pavement.

I stood and stared at my school, and my head began to pound. I couldn't believe it. How?! How did the school look so different? I'd won the competition back in sixth grade, which had changed *everything*. But now . . . now it just looked all *wrong*.

"Oh . . . no . . ." I said out loud, my throat tightening. "You've *got* to be kidding me."

CHAPTER 17
COMPETITION

Apart from Monster coming to live with us, the drawing competition was one of the best things that had ever happened to me. It was organized by a big supermarket chain, and every school across the country was invited to take part. There was a large cash prize for the overall winner: not for the kid—for their school.

The rules were simple: Draw or paint a picture of something in your town that makes you feel proud. Our school entered twenty pictures. I was quite pleased with mine, but to be honest, I'd forgotten about the whole thing until four months later when Mr. Howard came into our classroom all flustered, saying that I had reached the top ten. I thought he meant the top ten in our area, but he actually meant the top ten in the *whole country*.

There was a big awards ceremony, so me, Mr. Howard, Mum, Dad, and Bex all went on the train to the posh art gallery in London where it was taking place. When we arrived, we were taken on a tour of the gallery, which was really dull. First, the man taking us around kept droning on and on about the "light" and the "depth" and the "symbolism" in each painting. And second, the paintings weren't very good. In fact, they were rubbish. There was even one of an old sock! And it wasn't even a nice sock; it had holes in it and it looked like it was covered in dog hairs. While the guide was rambling on about the meaning behind the painting's title, *The Sock*, I nudged Mr. Howard.

"I'd have called it *The Stink* . . ." I whispered, creasing up with laughter, but Mr. Howard just rolled his eyes at me. He'd been in a mood all day and kept checking his mobile phone when he thought we weren't looking. I took a peek on the train and saw that he had a lot of texts from someone called "Clare H." I knew immediately who that was. It was my Spanish teacher—Ms. Huxley. It was obvious they had a thing for each other, but she was leaving at the end of the week to work in Australia.

After the boring tour, we went into a big room that had a stage at one end, and we found our seats in the second row, which had our names on them. A man wearing a shirt that was too tight around his neck started talking into a microphone about the competition and waving his arms. As he went on and on, I watched the top button on his shirt, waiting for it to burst off, but it didn't.

The top ten pictures had been put onto big wooden easels, and Mum tapped me on the arm and pointed at my drawing as if I didn't know which one I'd drawn. The man went on about art in schools and *blah, blah, blah*, and how this competition had shown that there were some really talented children out there and *blah, blah, blah*, and how creativity was so important and *blah, blah, blah*, and didn't we all do well? He then handed the microphone to a woman who he said was from the big supermarket, but she wasn't wearing a cashier's uniform; she was wearing a gray suit with bright pink high heels.

She had a big bunch of index cards that she kept looking at, and then it was her turn to go on and on. First, she said how wonderful her supermarket was and how they put so much back into their community and *waffle, waffle, waffle* . . . and then I started yawning so Dad nudged me in the ribs.

Eventually the woman got to her last index card and said it was time to announce the winner and could the finalists please make their way to the stage. I followed the other kids and we all stood next to our pictures. I got a closer look at what I was up against then, and there were some good ones. One girl had drawn her town's war memorial statue, and a boy, who must have lived in London, had done an aerial view of St Paul's Cathedral. I figure he must have copied that from somewhere unless he'd been up in a helicopter or something. Lady Supermarket began to talk again.

"It gives me great pleasure to announce that in third place, and winning art equipment for their school . . . is . . . Isobel Steele for her picture *Allotments* from her hometown in Devon!"

We all clapped as Isobel came forward. She shook the lady's hand and took an envelope, and then she started to cry, but I'm not sure if that was because she was so overwhelmed or just fed up that she hadn't come first.

"In second place, and winning art *and* sports equipment for their school . . . is . . . Benjamin Durrell—for his picture *Make Me Better.*"

Benjamin fist-punched the air and let out a "Yes!" as he made his way to receive his prize. As we clapped politely, I took a quick look at his picture. He'd drawn the outside of a hospital's emergency room, and through the windows you could see people covered in blood. It looked like there'd been some massive disaster. One man was clutching his shoulder, but his arm was missing and there was blood spurting out all over the floor. I'd bet Benjamin was into gaming quite a bit.

I looked over at Mum, Dad, Bex, and Mr. Howard. They all gave me a weak smile. There was no way I was going to win against *St Paul's Cathedral*, but it had been an okay day and I'd gotten out of going to school.

"So, now for the big one," said Lady Supermarket. "All our finalists have created some truly outstanding pieces of work, each one showing us what makes them proud to live where they do. But this person's choice was so original and had such *light* and *depth* and *symbolism* that it was actually a unanimous decision for the top prize."

The whole room fell silent.

"In first place and winning a complete makeover for their school up to the value of one hundred thousand pounds is . . . Maxwell Beckett, for his picture, wonderfully titled *Reg*."

I gulped. I'd won? I'd actually won? The audience erupted into applause, and Mum, Dad, Mr. Howard, and Bex shot up out of their seats and cheered. I was stunned. I made my way to Lady Supermarket, and she shook my hand and gave me an envelope, and then some flashes went off as someone started taking photographs. Lady Supermarket let me soak in the applause, and someone brought my picture to the front of the stage. When the clapping died down, Lady Supermarket began talking into the microphone again.

"Maxwell, can I ask you what made you choose this subject matter as something that you're proud of in your town?" She pointed the microphone toward me.

I shrugged.

"I dunno. I guess I like Reg, and he lives in my town . . . so that kind of makes me proud."

She grimaced a little as I answered, but she quickly turned it into a grin and started clapping. Everyone else applauded again. I ran down the steps and joined Mum, Dad, Bex, and Mr. Howard, and they all patted me on the back, and Mum and Dad gave me a big hug. It was incredible.

After we left the gallery, Dad suggested we go to one of those expensive burger places where you get your dinner on a wooden board rather than a plate. Even Mr. Howard came with us, which would normally have been really weird, but this time it was okay.

"I'm so proud of you, Maxwell. You've got real talent there. You've got to keep up the drawing," said Dad as he tucked into a chicken burger.

I smiled as I sucked on the straw in my chocolate milk shake.

"Yeah, well done, Max," said Bex, punching me lightly on the arm.

"I've phoned the school, and Mrs. Lloyd said they are going to make an announcement in assembly tomorrow," said Mr. Howard. "They've got big plans for the money already. The school is desperate for some renovations."

He was right. The playground was full of potholes, the ceiling of the auditorium leaked, and the classrooms were dark and shabby. Every now and then the walls were repainted, but it didn't really make much difference. But now it was going to change for the better, and it was all because of me.

Mum and Dad started talking about what train to get home,

and Mr. Howard got his phone out again. I took a peek over his shoulder and saw he had three text messages from Clare, aka Ms. Huxley. I couldn't read them all, but I caught the end of the last one: . . . *you can't even tell me how you feel?!!?* I'd seen Mr. Howard and Ms. Huxley hanging around together at school, sometimes in the playground and sometimes in the parking lot. They seemed to orbit around each other like there was some weird magnetic force pulling them together. But about a month earlier, they suddenly stopped hanging out so much, and Ms. Huxley announced at the end of our Spanish class that she was leaving to go work in Australia. Even though it sounded like a great big adventure, she didn't seem very happy about it. I had a feeling that her going away had something to do with Mr. Howard being so grumpy. He let out a long sigh, put his phone down on the table, and dropped his half-eaten veggie burger onto the plate.

"Mr. Howard?" I said. He wiped his mouth with his napkin and turned to me.

"Yes, Maxwell?" he said.

I put my burger down as well.

"You should tell her how you feel, you know."

Mr. Howard looked away and took a slurp of his Coke.

"What do you mean?" He spoke quietly so that Mum, Dad, and Bex couldn't hear.

"Ms. Huxley. She's going to Australia soon, isn't she?"

He nodded and his forehead creased up.

"I'm just saying you should tell her what she means to you. Before she leaves."

Mr. Howard shook his head.

"I don't think we need to discuss my private life. Do you, Maxwell?" he said.

We sat there in silence for a while as he fiddled with the straw in his glass. The ice cubes jingled around and around.

"Anyway," he continued, "she's made plans. She's paid for a flight and gotten a job. It's all been arranged. I can't compete with Australia. What do I have to offer?"

I was quite surprised he said that. From what I could tell, Mr. Howard was a very nice man indeed.

"Well, I don't know about that," I said. "But you teachers are always saying that honesty is the best policy, or whatever it is . . . so all you need to do is tell her the truth. Yeah? She needs to know the *facts* and *then* she can decide."

Mr. Howard thought about it for a bit and began to nod. He picked up his cell and stood up. "Excuse me, everyone, I just need to make a call."

I didn't need to ask Mr. Howard how it had gone. He sat on the train staring out of the window with a stupid grin on his face all the way home. Later that week there was a school announcement that Ms. Huxley had decided to stay at Green Mills High School after all, and that they would soon be starting work on important renovations, now that Maxwell Beckett had won some vital funds.

It took about ten months for all the work to be done, but the money I'd won turned the school from a shabby, run-down mess into a bright, clean, modern building.

———

I remembered all this as I stood gripping the cold iron railings that surrounded the school. My jaw dropped open and my mouth dried as I blinked at the sight in front of me.

I couldn't believe it.

Everything had gone back to how it used to be.

CHAPTER 18
SCHOOL

I pressed my forehead against the cold black bars as I stared at the school.

There were the two big doors that led to the main reception area. This was where I had sat just the other day, outside the principal's office, while Charlie had been making all that fuss about his nose. Beyond this was the staff room, some lockers, and the main auditorium.

But the reception area was . . . wrong . . .

One half of the double doors had been boarded up with a piece of old wood, and the paintwork on the window frames had completely peeled away. The sign next to the door should have read:

GREEN MILLS HIGH SCHOOL MAIN RECEPTION

But this sign said:

G EEN M LLS HIG S   OOL MA N ECEP ON

The first thing the school had done with the money I'd won was to smarten up the main entrance. They said they wanted the reception to be a clean, welcoming area for students, staff, and visitors. They'd changed the windows, replaced the doors, and fixed a shiny new school sign to the wall. But now . . . it was all back to exactly how it was before.

On the glass of the door that wasn't broken was a poster:

CENTENARY FUND-RAISING RAFFLE

HELP US CELEBRATE REACHING 100 YEARS BY SELLING RAFFLE TICKETS!

(ALL MONEY RAISED WILL GO TOWARD VITAL SCHOOL RENOVATIONS.)

I read the poster three times. What raffle? The school was having a ball with a TV crew to celebrate being one hundred years old, not a boring raffle!

The gate was open, so I walked in and around to the side of the auditorium with the huge glass windows. This was where Jed and Baz had presented the start of their roadshow before I'd humiliated myself and ruined it for everyone. Most of the money had been spent on the main auditorium because it had been pretty unusable. If it rained, the place was completely out-of-bounds because the floor would be dotted with orange buckets catching water from the holes in the roof.

I walked over to the tall windows, circled my hands around my eyes, and looked in.

I gasped.

The auditorium was filled with orange buckets.

Hundreds of them.

All ready to catch any rain that came through the roof.

The stage area, where Charlie Geek had stood waiting to play Jed and Baz's version of Pin the Tail on the Donkey, used to be a no-go area. I looked toward the stage now. Across the front there was a rope with a sign pegged to the middle that read: STRICTLY NO ACCESS. I stepped away. Nothing had been repaired at all. My heart pounded as I walked back to the gate. I was frightened and I was confused and I certainly didn't want to see any more.

"Hey, you! What do you think you're doing?"

I looked up. There was one car parked in the staff lot, and a man was shouting out of the window. I froze.

"You're not supposed to be on school property on a Sunday," he shouted again. It was Mr. Howard. He had a sandwich in his hand.

I stood there for a moment and stared at him while he stared back at me. Did he recognize me? And what was he doing here on a Sunday, sitting in his car, eating a sandwich?

"Sorry, sir," I said, and I put my head down and carried on walking. After a few paces I stopped and turned around, and then I headed straight for Mr. Howard's car. I had to be certain about what was going on here, once and for all.

I stood by the passenger window. My homeroom teacher looked up at me, his eyes wide. Pieces of cheese had fallen out of his sandwich onto his lap, and his hair was all over the place. On one side of his shirt there was a stain that looked like coffee. He didn't look neat like he usually did. He glared back at me and then he lowered the window.

"Can I help you?" he said.

"I'm sorry I'm on school property, Mr. Howard," I said. "I had to check something out. Something really important."

Mr. Howard studied my face.

"I see. And what might that be?"

There was a cardboard cup on the dashboard, and he picked it up and slurped from it.

"I—I wanted to see how the auditorium was looking and if the buckets were in position and ready for the rain tonight."

He nodded.

"And is there going to be rain tonight?"

I shrugged.

"I dunno. But I thought I'd better check. You know. Just in case."

As I spoke, I turned my face this way and that so he could get a good look at me, but I think it just made me look a bit weird.

"Well. Now that you've done your checking, you'd better head home."

He frowned. I knew he was trying to place me. I just knew it.

"Why are you here on a Sunday, sir?"

Mr. Howard went to take a big bite of his sandwich, then stopped.

"I didn't have any plans . . . so I thought I'd come here and catch up with some work."

I frowned.

"In your car?" I said.

Mr. Howard blinked at me.

"The staff room feels too . . . empty," he said. His eyes went a bit watery, and then he shook himself out of it. "Anyway, this is none of your business now, is it, er, um . . ."

I blinked at him. *Say it! It's Maxwell! Just say it! I'm in your class every day. Please say it!*

He took a big bite of his sandwich as he studied my face.

"Whose class are you in again?" he said through a mouthful of food.

My heart shriveled to the size of an acorn. He didn't know

me. Mr. Howard, my very own homeroom teacher, had no idea who I was.

"I . . . I've got to go," I said, and I turned and ran out of the lot.

———————

For the rest of the day I walked. I walked for miles and miles and miles. I wanted to see everything, to check on everything that I'd ever done. And the first place I checked was the swimming pool.

CHAPTER 19
POOL

Every Sunday morning when we were little, Mum and Dad would take me and Bex to Family Fun Swim. Our local pool would be transformed with brightly colored inflatables and large foam floats, and we'd jump in with all the other families. Dad came up with this game where he pretended he was a hungry shark and wanted to eat us. We'd start at the side of the pool, and he'd count to ten while Bex, Mum, and I swam off toward the floats to try and reach safety before Dad snapped at our ankles. Mum was a slow swimmer, so Bex and I would get to the float first and clamber up, squealing at Mum to hurry up because Dad was right behind her. When Mum got to the float, she would laugh so much she couldn't pull herself out of the water. Dad would slide up beside her with his hand over his head like a shark's fin.

"Hmmm, someone looks tasty . . . Yum, yum, yum!" he'd say, and pretend to chomp on Mum's shoulder.

"Stop making me laugh, Eddie! I'm trying to get on the float! Give me a push up!"

Bex and I would help heave Mum onto the float, and then Dad would duck under the water and bang against the bottom, making us all squeal again.

That was a good memory. One of the best, in fact. I must have only been around seven. That was when they used to like each other and before they started arguing and putting stupid Post-its on their food. I can't even remember when it all changed. They just seemed to start getting on each other's nerves all the time, and it never got better.

———————

When I got to the swimming pool, the parking lot was really busy. I hadn't been there in years. There were loads of excited kids around wearing little backpacks, and I saw one girl was already wearing her goggles. I remembered doing that in the car on the way there. It made everyone laugh.

After one of our Family Fun Swim sessions, Dad, Bex, and I waited outside the pool while Mum got in line for milk shakes in the café. It was a hot, sunny day—too hot to sit in the car, so the three of us perched on the low redbrick wall that surrounded the parking lot. While we waited, Dad checked his phone and Bex weaved her damp hair into two braids. I was bored, so I climbed onto the wall and began to walk along. Dad glanced up at me.

"Be careful, Maxwell," he said, looking back down at his phone.

I walked along with my arms stretched out at my sides to help with my balance. Back then the wall had felt quite high and I took my time reaching the end. There were brown square tiles cemented on the top of the wall, and when I reached the corner, I went to turn back, but a tile beneath my foot wobbled and crashed to the concrete floor. I looked down. It had broken into five pieces. I waited for Dad to yell, but he was still scrolling through his phone and Bex was still braiding her hair; they hadn't heard a thing. I was worried I'd get into trouble, so I jumped down from the wall and quickly picked up the pieces and hid them underneath a bush. I was just standing up when a voice shouted across the parking lot.

"Maxwell! Milk shake!"

Mum was standing by Dad and Bex and waving a pink cup at me. I skipped back to my family and never told them what had happened to the tile.

We went to the swimming pool every Sunday for quite a while, and every now and then I took a quick walk along the wall to see if the broken tile had been replaced. It never had. In fact, no one ever seemed to notice that it had gone missing.

Now it was time to take another look.

I stood by the automatic door of the swimming pool, far enough away so it didn't keep opening but close enough to make it look like I was just waiting for someone. I pretended to check my watch by looking at my bare wrist, and then I began to walk along the wall that I used to balance on all those years ago. This time I didn't need to put my arms out at my sides.

A baby was crying as its mum took it out of its car seat, and a man with huge shoulders was padlocking his bike to a stand. I stared at my feet as I walked. Under my breath I whispered to myself, "Please be missing. Please be missing."

I reached the end of the wall, and then I took a deep breath and looked.

I shivered.

It was there.

The end tile that I'd knocked off and smashed into five pieces was back and completely unbroken.

It was just as if I had never been there to break it in the first place.

I jumped off the wall and touched the tile. It wobbled, exactly as it had when I'd accidentally knocked it off. I crouched down by the bush where I'd hidden the pieces and took a look. Maybe they'd finally gotten around to replacing the tile, but the broken pieces of the old one would still be under the bush?

All I found were three empty cans and a deflated water wing. There was no broken tile.

I sat on the wall and tried to think, but my head felt woozy.

Everything I'd done in the past had been . . . undone. The gate, the school, and now this. I got up. I didn't know what to do, so I began walking. I didn't really know where to go, so I just walked around, up and down roads that I knew so well.

I found myself on Acacia Drive. A couple of years ago, the town planted a little tree along the edge of the pavement. Within a week of it being there, I'd accidentally crashed my bike straight into it and snapped it in two. The broken tree had stayed there for months, slowly rotting away, until eventually someone came and dug it up, cementing over the little hole where it had been planted. But when I passed the spot now, the tree was there, three times my height with a scattering of red leaves circling the ground around it. I stopped and stared at it for a moment, and then I carried on.

Not far from my elementary school was a house that had a garden surrounded by an orangey-brown fence, the kind of fence that had solid panels that you couldn't see through. One day, on our way home from school, Mum bumped into her friend Kimberly. They stood talking for ages and ages, even though I tried tugging at my mum's coat to make her hurry up. As I waited, I ran my hand along the orangey-brown fence and touched a knot of wood, which looked like a large, staring eye. I pressed it, and the circle of wood popped out and fell through to the other side. While Mum wasn't watching, I quickly looked through the hole, gazing in at the hidden garden, which turned out to be just a jumble of brambles. I passed that fence twice a day for years and took a peek through the hole every now and then. As I passed the brown fence now, the circular knot of wood was back.

I put my hands in my pockets as I walked. Then I remembered there should be something there—the key to the boiler room that I'd locked on the night of the Hundredth Anniversary Celebration. But my pocket was empty. I walked and walked, and by late afternoon my feet were throbbing and I could barely put one foot in front of the other. I began to make my way back to Reg's.

I'd tried so hard to make sense of everything, to find a rational explanation for what was going on. But it was quite obvious that I was wrong. There was no hoax. My family wasn't behind any elaborate trick to try and teach me a lesson.

Something far worse had happened.

I, Maxwell Beckett, had been erased.

CHAPTER 20
SOUP

When I got back to Reg's, he was in the kitchen opening a can of tomato soup.

"Hello," he said as I appeared through the door. "Was I expecting you?"

For once I was grateful that Reg had forgotten me. After my earlier outburst with the cabinet, he might not have been so friendly if he'd remembered who I was. I explained as simply as I could that I was his friend, and then he invited me to have some dinner. My stomach was churning, and even though I didn't feel hungry, I knew I should probably eat something.

He told me to go and sit in the front room and wait while he finished cooking.

Once in the living room, I went straight to the glass cabinet. Reg had put all the things back neatly on the shelves. I felt goose bumps tickle up my arms. The cabinet freaked me out a little. Had something in there caused me to be erased? I carefully opened the door and looked inside. The wooden egg that I thought had broken when I pulled everything out was back in one piece on the shelf by the black hat. I picked it up. I remembered holding it the night before and turning it over in my hands, and I remembered it making a little noise. I shook it again and heard a rattle.

On top of the egg was a tiny wooden knob. I twisted it both ways. The knob moved, but nothing happened. Then I pressed it inward. There was a tiny click, and the egg suddenly popped open, four sides dropping down like petals on a flower. "What the . . . ?" I said, looking inside. A few things fell out onto the floor. I left them there for a moment as I studied the petals of the egg. Each one had some letters carved into the wood. I twisted the egg around and read.

"*M. Celeste, Amundsen, Louis Le Prince, Earhart,*" I said. "What does that mean?"

I got down onto my knees and looked at the things that had fallen out. There was a small square of thick dirty-white fabric, a silver button, a piece of knitted wool, and a folded handkerchief. I unfolded the handkerchief and saw that embroidered in one corner were the initials *A. E.*

"Are you ready for your soup, Maxwell?" called Reg from the kitchen.

"Yes, Reg," I replied.

I quickly picked everything up and stuffed it all back into the middle of the egg. I held each petal and folded them up around the bits in the middle. It clicked shut and was in the shape of an egg again. I put it on the shelf and made my way to the sofa.

"Here we go," said Reg, coming into the living room with a tray that he put on my knees.

"Where did that egg come from, Reg?" I said. "The wooden one that you said was a music box?" I blew on my soup and slurped at it.

"Oh, that old thing! My grandfather won it in a card game in Vietnam. He was always getting himself into scrapes and whatnot. Did I tell you he traveled the world three times?"

He chuckled to himself, and then he shuffled off to the kitchen again and came back with two thick slices of bread and butter. I was so tired. My feet throbbed from all the walking.

"Reg? What would you do if you didn't exist anymore?" I said, dunking my bread into my soup.

Reg stared at me.

"Is that a trick question?" he asked.

"No, it's not a trick. I just wondered how you would spend your time."

Reg thought about it for a moment.

"Well, if I didn't exist, I wouldn't do anything. I wouldn't be able to because I didn't exist."

I frowned.

"No, what I mean is . . . what if you *used* to exist, but something happened . . . some kind of magic . . . and you were erased from the world. You were still alive . . . still walking, talking, breathing, and in the town where you lived . . . but you'd never actually been born. And all the people you know, well, they now have no idea who you are. You've never existed."

Reg froze with a spoonful of steaming soup in front of his lips. He appeared to be giving it a great deal of thought. He blew gently on the soup.

"I think if that had happened, if I was still me and no one knew who I was . . . but I knew who *they* were . . . Well, I think I'd go and have a little fun," he said. A wide smile spread across his face.

"Fun?" I said. I couldn't think of anything fun about being me at the moment. Reg sipped his soup.

"Yes! It would be a bit like being invisible, don't you think?

You'd know all the people around you and all their secrets and habits and so on, but they wouldn't have a clue who you were." He slurped from the spoon. "No one would know your faults or your mistakes. You could be whoever you wanted to be."

I sat back on the sofa, my eyes drooping with tiredness. I was exhausted, but I felt a little calmer. My tummy was full, I was warm, and I had a roof over my head. Maybe Reg was right. Maybe not existing wasn't such a bad thing after all. I'd made such a mess of my old life and upset a lot of people. Maybe I would have more luck in this world. Here, nobody hated me or thought I was a trouble-maker or a total loser. I hadn't made *any* mistakes. My family was probably around somewhere, so I just had to find them and work out a way to get back into their lives.

I leaned into the plump pillows on the sofa. I let my eyes close for a moment. Charlie Geek was here in this world, and I was certain I'd be able to be friends with him again. A better friend this time, too. That shouldn't be too hard. As I rested, I felt Reg lift my tray off my lap and heard him head to the kitchen.

I smiled to myself.

Maybe, in this world, Maxwell Beckett could do better.

CHAPTER 21
STATION

The next morning, I woke up feeling surprisingly relaxed. Reg must have put the blanket over me before he went to bed, and he'd left the gas fire on low. When he came into the living room wearing blue-striped pajamas, he did a little jump when he saw me.

"What on earth are you doing on my sofa?" he said. We went through the usual questions, although this time he seemed to understand a bit quicker. This time I told him that my parents were friends of his, that they'd had to go away for work, and that he'd agreed to look after me for a bit.

"They told you not to forget and that it was very important that you let me stay. Don't you remember, Reg?" I said.

I felt guilty for lying to him again. He looked a bit anxious, but then he pretended he did remember and it was fine for me to stay. He went off to the kitchen and came back with four slices of toast and jam on a plate as I lay under my blanket.

"Thanks, Reg," I said. This was quite nice. I usually had to wait until I heard Dad leave to do his job as a gardener before I got up. If one of them was out of the way, then there'd be no arguing.

"What time does school start for you, then, young Maxwell?" Reg asked, sitting down in his armchair and resting a white bowl on his tummy. It was full to the brim with cornflakes.

"There's, um, no school this week, Reg. It's . . . fall break. Mum told you that already."

He looked a bit embarrassed and then nodded and smiled.

"Oh yes, of course. Your parents . . . you're staying with me for a while, aren't you?"

I smiled back, though I felt bad. It wasn't the school break, but Reg would never find that out, and I didn't think it was too bad telling him a white lie. Besides, the alternative was far too complicated.

As I ate my toast, I thought about my plan for the day. I knew exactly what I was going to do.

Today I was going to find my family, and I was going to find Monster.

———

Reg had run out of milk, so I offered to go and get some. The nearest shop was a mini-supermarket next to the train station about half a mile away. It was a bright, crisp autumn morning, and Mrs. Banks was making her way along her stepping stones carrying her trash can—the can that Monster loved to have a good old snuffle through. My stomach leaped as I thought about him. I couldn't wait to kiss his velvety ears and see his funny helicopter tail going mad when he saw me! I bet he would know who I was instantly, because of our special bond.

Mrs. Banks dumped her can onto the pavement. I suddenly thought that she might have an idea where Monster might be living.

"Um, excuse me," I said. She glared at me through her sweeping bangs. "Have you seen a beagle around here at all? With a tongue that hangs out all the time?"

I was expecting some snide comment, but she actually seemed to be thinking about it.

"I can't say that I have. Have you lost him?"

I nodded. "Kind of," I said.

"That's a shame," she said. "Maybe you should put up some posters."

I couldn't believe it. She was actually being nice.

"Um, yes . . . Okay. Maybe I should do that," I said, watching her carefully.

"You could put one on my gate if you like. Lots of people stop by here to admire my garden," she said proudly.

I'd never heard her speak kindly before. It was strange. We both stood for a moment and looked at the garden.

"Nice flamingo," I said, to break the silence.

Mrs. Banks glanced toward the bird, which was pinker than ever in the bright sun.

"Oh, thank you," she said. And then her lips did this weird thing. The corners slowly curled upward and she smiled. I'd never seen her smile. I was so shocked, I burst out laughing. Her smile dropped instantly and was replaced with a scowl. She folded her arms and glared at me.

"Aren't you supposed to be in school uniform?" she said.

"Day off," I said, and I quickly carried on.

It might not have lasted long, but that was the nicest conversation I had ever had with Mrs. Banks. She didn't hate me! Maybe Reg was right. I could be whoever I wanted to be in this world and nobody hated me.

When I got to the shop, there were hundreds of commuters

rushing toward the station entrance, fumbling with their tickets. A woman pushed past me, talking loudly on her cell phone so that everyone could hear her conversation.

"If Madrid wants to sell it at that price, then I think we should grab it with both hands. Don't you, Damien?"

I wondered what Madrid was selling. Whatever it was, it must have been quite big, because it needed two hands to hold it. The woman swept through the ticket hall, managing to not bump into anyone as she twisted her body through the crowds.

A bus pulled up, and a jumble of suits and elbows emerged from the doors and rushed toward the station. A large group was coming from the parking lot in the other direction, and as the two crowds met, a man in a navy suit stumbled and his phone shot out of his hand and went spinning across the pavement. It came to a stop beside my foot. I picked it up just as the image on the shattered screen died. I held on to the phone, still staring at it. My heart rate quickened. I recognized that photograph! It was of a girl holding cotton candy and sitting at the top of a Ferris wheel. However, this version was a bit different. In the version I knew, there was a boy sitting next to her pulling a stupid face and basically ruining the whole picture. I took a deep breath as a pair of shiny black shoes appeared in front of me.

"Can I have my phone?"

I looked up and swallowed. It was my dad. He was standing right there. I stared at his face, but he just looked blank. He didn't know me at all.

"I . . . er . . . um," I stuttered. My dad rolled his eyes and held out his hand.

"My phone? Please? Come on, I'm in a hurry."

I gave it to him, and when he saw the smashed screen, his shoulders slumped.

"Oh, that's just terrific. A flat tire and now this. Can my day get any worse? Can it?"

He looked straight at me, his forehead crumpled. He appeared to be waiting for an answer. I shrugged.

"I dunno. Maybe?" I said.

He sighed, glanced at his watch, and then turned and did a weird running-while-trying-to-look-like-walking thing toward the station entrance. I hadn't seen him looking so dressed up since . . . well, since back when I was in primary school and he used to work in London in the busy office. The one that made him really ill.

———

Back then we were rich. Well, not rich exactly, but I never saw Mum's face drop when I told her there was a school trip to pay for or that my shoes were getting too tight. Back then we could easily afford everyday stuff and we even went to Greece a couple of times. That was all because Dad used to get a bonus, which meant the company he worked for would put a great chunk of money straight into his bank account every year. But then, one day, Dad stopped going to work. Just like that. It was like he woke up one morning and couldn't find the energy to get out of bed, so he just decided to stay there.

Mum spent a lot of time whispering on the phone, and she made him an appointment to see a doctor. The doctor gave Dad a prescription for pills, and once a week he went to see another type of doctor named Cathy. He went to see Cathy to "talk about things." I don't know what they talked about, but after a few weeks, he stopped spending so much time in bed and started to do stuff again. He really loved being outside, so one day I helped him to dig our little vegetable patch in the garden. When I say "helped," I mean I just stood there asking questions while he did all the work. I was only about six, so I probably wouldn't have been very good at it anyway.

I remember asking him about worms and which end was their head and which end was their bottom.

"I don't know, Maxwell," he said with a laugh. "You'll have to look that one up."

He stabbed his spade into the ground and it made a *clunk* sound. He bent down and moved some of the soil out of the way with his hands, and then he picked up a piece of red brick. He dusted the dirt off it.

"You know, Maxwell, Cathy said something to me the other day that really made me think," he said, staring at the brick. "She said that having a worry or an upset or a sense of loss can feel like you are carrying a really heavy brick in your pocket."

I watched him silently as he crouched down, looking at the lump in his hand.

"She said that some days that brick can feel like the heaviest brick in the whole wide world. It's so heavy in your pocket that you can barely put one foot in front of the other."

He stood up, still looking at the brick.

"But some days the worry that you are carrying around with you is still there, like a brick in your pocket, but you might not notice it as much. That brick just doesn't feel as heavy as it used to."

I frowned. It might have made sense to Dad, but it didn't make any sense to me. He tossed the brick to one side, then carried on digging. I watched him for a bit, thinking.

"Daddy?" I said. "When are you going back to your job?"

He stopped again and sort of froze like a statue. I thought I might have said something really wrong, but then he straightened up and wiped his forehead.

"Soon, Maxwell. In a couple of weeks, I'd say."

He carried on digging, and I noticed his face was all scrunched up. I kicked at the ground and spotted a big pebble. It was all white and smooth, and I brushed the dirt off and put it into my pocket. I looked back at my dad. His cheeks were flushed and his eyes looked all watery.

"Daddy? Why do you do a job that you don't like very much?"

He stopped digging and stood the spade up in front of him, resting his hands on the top of the handle. He wiped his forehead, then looked straight at me, giving me a little smile.

"Do you know something, Maxwell? I don't really know." He stood for a while, staring ahead. It was quite boring just watching him do nothing, so I ran off to put the white pebble on the shelf in my bedroom.

Not long after that, Dad announced that he wasn't going back to his old job after all. He said what was the point of doing a job he didn't like? And then he gave me a really big smile. Dad went to college to learn about horticulture, which is all about plants and stuff. He said he really wanted to be a gardener. Mum explained that we'd have a lot less money, but it was important that adults tried to do jobs that they enjoy. She said they spend a lot of their lives at work, and that Dad's old job was making him very unhappy. He worked in a pub in the evenings and studied really hard in the daytime, and he passed all his exams. Eventually he bought a van and set up his own business: Eddie's Gardening Services. He was happy again.

———————

I watched as this other version of my dad made his way through the crowds. In this world, it looked like he was still working in his stressful office job in London. Did that mean he was going to get ill again? Why hadn't he gone back to college to learn about plants and gardening? I watched as the back of his head disappeared in the crowd, and then I stood up and headed to the store to buy the milk.

CHAPTER 22
WAITING

Reg told me I could keep the change from the milk money, so I bought myself a cheap toothbrush. I was quite proud of myself for being sensible and choosing something I actually needed. If I'd been in my old world, I'd have just chosen candy. This was all working out fine, and I decided to carry on with being the new me when I got back to Reg's.

"Can I help you with any jobs while I'm staying here, Reg?" I asked.

Reg thought for a moment, and then his eyes lit up.

"As a matter of fact, you can!" he said.

I grinned back, but to be honest I was hoping he'd say no and we could just sit around on the sofa and watch TV. Now that I knew Dad was still in the area, I planned to see if I could find Bex after school, but that was hours away.

Reg asked me to help him get the living room curtains down so that he could give them a wash. I stood on a chair and worked out how they came off as Reg held the curtain below until he had the whole lot in his arms. After that I did the vacuuming while Reg went around waving a yellow duster at things. We had lunch, and then Reg sat in his armchair and chatted while I cleaned the insides of his windows.

"You are a thoughtful boy, Maxwell. Thank you."

I squirted the glass with some spray, then wiped it with a

cloth. I smiled. No one had ever called me thoughtful before. All this "being nice" business was hard, though. The windows kept going smeary, so I folded and refolded the cloth a few times and tried again. After I finished, I turned around and saw that Reg had nodded off in his chair. It was just after three o'clock. Time to try and find Bex.

I got to school at 3:25 p.m. and got in position behind a tree. At exactly three thirty, the bell blasted for the end of school, and within five seconds the main doors burst open and hundreds of kids in navy uniforms spilled across the playground. I checked all the faces, trying to spot Bex, but there was no sign of her. I recognized a few kids from my class, including Marcus Grundy. He had another boy in a headlock and was walking along with him like he was carrying a bag under his arm. There weren't any teachers around to see.

"Get off, Marcus!" the boy shouted. It was Charlie Geek. Marcus looked around, pretending he didn't know where the voice was coming from.

"Marcus! Let me go!" Charlie yelled again. Marcus shrugged his shoulders, and the kids around him began to laugh.

"Hey, you!" I shouted, coming out from behind the tree and walking right up to the fence. "Let him go, you idiot!"

Charlie tried to look up, but he couldn't move his head.

"Who says?" said Marcus, snarling at me.

"Me!" I shouted. Unlike everyone else, I wasn't frightened of Marcus Grundy. I never had been. He took a few steps toward me with Charlie still in a headlock. A small crowd began to gather around.

"Why don't you come over here and make me, eh?" said Marcus. I looked up and saw Mr. Townsend, one of the science teachers, coming out of the main doors.

I leaned closer to the fence.

"If you don't let him go, I'll tell everyone what you did in your pants in first grade. Remember the flowerpot, Marcus?"

A few people around him spluttered and began to laugh.

"What was that? What did he say about your pants?" said Charlie, from his awkward angle. Marcus tightened his grip, but I noticed his face had gone pale.

"But how? How did you know about that?" he whispered. I grinned back at him and tapped the side of my forehead with one finger.

Marcus's mum used to meet my mum for coffee when we were in primary school. One evening I overheard her telling Dad something that Marcus's mum had told her. Apparently he had had an "accident" in his pants in school, and rather than own up and tell the teacher he hadn't gotten to the toilet in time, he tried to discreetly fish it out and dump it in a plant pot in the corner of the classroom. The teacher spotted what he was doing before anyone noticed and told him to go to the bathroom. The story never got out. I'd known all about Marcus's little poo incident for seven years now, and I'd carefully stored it away in my brain to use in case of emergency. That time was now.

"What was that about a flowerpot?" said Sanjeev Howe.

Marcus let Charlie go, and he slowly stood upright, rubbing the back of his neck.

"Yeah, tell us all about it!" snorted Ebony Garland. "We are dying to know." She'd had a tough time from Marcus in the past, so she seemed especially pleased with how uncomfortable he was looking. Mr. Townsend came over to see what was going on, and I dropped back near the tree again.

"There you go, buddy. No harm done, eh?" said Marcus, brushing invisible dust from Charlie's shoulders as the teacher arrived. "I'll knock for you in the morning?"

Charlie nodded. "Yeah, okay. See you tomorrow, Marcus."

I couldn't believe it. They were *friends*? Charlie and Marcus? That was ridiculous! Charlie was fiddling with his hair and trying to get it to stick up again after it been flattened by the headlock. Now I came to think of it, Charlie's hair was *exactly* the same as Marcus's. He was even trying to look like him!

I checked my watch: 3:39 p.m. I quickly scanned the playground, but there was still no sign of Bex. Maybe she didn't go to this school anymore. What would I do then? How would I find her, Mum, and Monster if she wasn't here?

I spotted some girls from her year, including Claudia Bradwell, the girl who had been cruel about Bex's outfit at the ball. Everyone was leaving, and before long there were just two boys left kicking a stone around until a teacher yelled at them to make their way home. There weren't any clubs at school on Mondays. Where was she? A voice behind me suddenly made me jump.

"Who are you, and what do you want?"

I turned around and faced Charlie Geek. He was gripping the strap of his backpack on his shoulder and scowling. It was his "trying to be brave" look.

"Charlie!" I said. "How are you?" I gave him my best,

friendliest grin, trying not to stare too much at his hair. The school badge on his blazer was hanging off where the stitching had been unpicked. Marcus's was like that, too.

"Why are you following me around? You came to my house and now you're at my school. What do you want?" He looked around nervously. "Are you from *Prank Me Out*?"

Prank Me Out is a show on TV where you set your friends up to look stupid and it's supposed to be funny. There was one episode where there was this boy who secretly wanted to be a pop star. They hid cameras in his bedroom and filmed him singing into a comb while watching himself in the mirror. The following day he went to the movies with his friends and, instead of the film coming on to the screen, the *Prank Me Out* team played the clip of him singing in his room. His friends, who had set him up, found it hilarious, and the whole theater screamed with laughter. The boy laughed along, too, but you could tell from his face that he was actually trying not to cry.

"What do you think I am? *Prank Me Out*?! No! I'd *never* do that," I said. "I hate that program as much as you do!"

Charlie looked baffled.

"But . . . how do you know I hate *Prank Me Out*?"

"I'm just . . . I . . . um," I stuttered. "Everyone hates it, don't they?"

"Who are you?" said Charlie, taking a step closer and folding his arms. I suddenly had an idea. "We went to the same nursery school. Remember? We were great friends and we played together *all* the time!"

The problem with this was that we didn't actually go to the

same nursery school. I had no idea where he went, and I could barely remember where I had gone.

"We did?" he said, looking up to the left as he tried to find a memory of me. "What did we do there?"

I jiggled about on the spot a bit.

"Ohhh, well, we played with the Play-Doh . . . and, um, in the home area with the little wooden kitchen . . . and, oh! I know! We used to drive around in those big plastic cars where you had to push yourself with your feet."

Charlie smiled.

"I *loved* those cars," he said.

"Yeah, me too!" I said, slapping him on the arm. "The teacher . . . old, um, what's-her-name, she couldn't get us out of them! Do you remember?"

Charlie nodded, but he still looked puzzled. "What was your name again?" he said.

"Maxwell," I said. Charlie rubbed his lip with his finger, thinking. "Anyway, none of that matters. I was in your past and now . . . I'm back! *I* remember you, and *you've* forgotten me. But, you know. It's no biggie . . ." I shrugged and stuck out my bottom lip. Charlie looked really uncomfortable then. Making him feel like he'd upset me so that I got my own way was one of my most-used skills. He was still frowning.

"B-but I really don't remember you. At *all*," he said. He looked a bit upset about it now, so I gave him a beaming smile.

"Don't worry about it. I'm not offended!" I said, whacking him on the arm again. "Look, you don't happen to know a girl named Bex in tenth grade, do you?"

Charlie sniffed.

"Bex Beckett? Yeah, of course I do. Everyone knows her," he said. My sister was always going up in assembly, picking up awards for Best History Project or Most Successful Student of the Term and that kind of rubbish. Of course he would know who she was.

"Do you know where she is?" I asked.

"Oh, she'll be ages yet. Detention doesn't finish for another twenty minutes."

"What?!" I choked. "What do you mean, detention?"

"Bex Beckett has been in permanent detention ever since she started a fire in the art room garbage can at the beginning of term. The whole school was evacuated and six fire engines turned up! I'm surprised she hasn't been suspended again, to be honest."

"Suspended?! *Again?!*" I said.

"Yeah. Her crowd is pretty much out of control," said Charlie, rolling his eyes. "Her friend Claudia Bradwell is just as bad. Anyway, I gotta go. See you later."

And then he turned and headed off down the road.

CHAPTER 23
BEX

This didn't sound like my sister at all. And Bex was friends with Claudia after everything she'd done? That couldn't be right. Charlie must have been exaggerating. Surely Bex wasn't that bad, was she? I knew my sister, and that really didn't sound like her at *all*.

I checked my watch. Twenty minutes was up. Bex would be out any moment now. I decided that it would probably be best if I just followed her and found out where she lived. Then I could see if Mum was okay and give Monster a really big hug. I wasn't sure how I was going to do that bit, but I really, really wanted to see my dog. I leaned against the tree and watched as an empty chip bag blew around the playground. It swooped gently, this way and that, almost as if it couldn't decide which way to go. I watched the bag blow toward the main gate. Suddenly a foot wearing a brown boot stamped down on top of it like it was crushing a butterfly. My jaw dropped when I saw who the leg belonged to.

It was Bex. Her long brown hair was pulled into a really high ponytail. It was so tight, she had a shocked look in her eyes. Her school tie was twisted so that only the smaller bit showed. You got an automatic detention if you did that, but considering she was already *in* detention, it probably wasn't going to make much difference. She was wearing black skinny jeans instead of the regulation school trousers and, more shockingly, she appeared to be wearing about two inches of thick orange makeup. I watched, dumbstruck, as she turned left and headed down the road.

I started to follow. I kept my distance, but it wouldn't have made much difference as she was too busy scrolling through her phone to notice me.

When she got to the main street, she went into a shop called Candy Lashes. Underneath the shop sign, which was written in bright purple bubble letters, it said: *Accessorize 4 Life*. I looked through the window and was faced with piles and piles of stuff. There were brushes and bows and clips and slides and long pieces of hair that looked like they had been snipped off someone's head. There was also a row of jewelry and a wall full of makeup. I stood by the window. This was a shop that Bex would never, ever go in.

A woman behind the counter smiled at Bex and then carried on serving a customer. I watched as my sister picked up a sparkly purse and studied it for a bit, turning it over in her hands. My stomach tightened as she looked over at the shop assistant, and then it relaxed as Bex put the purse back. She made her way toward the makeup section. I stepped to the side so that I had a better view as she picked up a bottle of perfume, squirted it onto her wrist, gave it a sniff, and then put it back. She then chose some pink, sparkly nail polish and looked at the tiny label on the bottle. She put her hand up to scratch her head and *poof*, as if by magic the bottle disappeared.

"What the heck . . . ?" I said, squinting at the floor to try and see where it had gone.

Bex picked up another one, a green color this time, held it as if she was looking for the price, scratched her nose, and *poof*, it vanished just like the pink one. This time I saw exactly where it had gone; she had dropped it down the sleeve of her school blazer. Her fingers gripped the cuff so that the bottles didn't drop out onto the floor. She chose one more bottle, a blue one this time, and *abracadabra*, that disappeared, too. She was like a thieving magician. She glanced around the shop one last time, then stuffed both of her hands into her blazer pockets and walked quickly toward the door. I turned away so she didn't see me, and then I followed her as she headed down the street.

My goody-two-shoes sister was a thief! I couldn't believe it! She crossed the road and I did the same, keeping a few paces behind her. What was she thinking? Did she not realize how much trouble she could get into if she was caught? We got to the outside of the library when she suddenly stopped and turned around.

"Why are you following me?" she said. Her nose was scrunched up and her eyes were narrowed to slits.

"Bex!" I stuttered. She looked even more orange close up.

"How do you know my name? Do you go to my school?"

I cleared my throat.

"Um . . . yes," I said.

She narrowed her eyes so much they were nearly closed.

"Well? What do you want?" she said.

I jiggled around a bit.

"I'm just . . . I . . . um. I'm doing a survey . . . for school . . . for homework. I wanted to ask you a question."

She glared at me again.

"Look. I'm not in the mood for stupid games. Okay?" She dropped a shoulder one way and cocked her head the other, and then she spun around, and I watched her ponytail bob away as she headed down the street.

"Bex! Wait up," I said, chasing after her. She turned around and huffed and rolled her eyes all at the same time.

"Can you just answer a question for my homework? Please? Otherwise I'll get into big trouble."

She sniffed and stared at the ground.

"Okay. What is your stupid question?" she said.

"Um. Well . . . it's, um . . . What breed of dog do you own?"

She frowned. "Is that it?" she said.

I tried to look serious.

"Yes. We're doing a project on . . . um . . . dogs in the community for, um . . . Geography."

Bex rolled her eyes again. Eye-rolling seemed to be her thing.

"I don't have a dog. Never have. Never will. Does that answer your question? Now go away."

She carried on walking. I skipped along beside her.

"You don't have a beagle? A beagle that likes eating? He's about this high," I said, putting my hand down at my knee level. "And he smells a bit. Especially his breath. And he's called Monster. Or any name, really. Any name you might have called him. Forget about the Monster bit . . . You probably called him something else, like Einstein or Napoleon, knowing you . . ."

She glanced at me then and pulled a confused face, but she didn't say anything. We walked along in silence for a bit, and when she realized I wasn't going away she stopped.

"Look, weirdo, get lost! Got that?" she said.

"But you haven't answered me properly! About the dog!" I said. She folded her arms.

"I think I'd know if I had a dog or not, don't you?" she said. "Anyway, what is your problem? Are you a freak or something?"

I blinked back at her. I couldn't believe it. She didn't have a dog. A terrible realization hit me. How could I have been so stupid? If I had never been born, then of course I wouldn't have been there on that day to save Monster. The day when he was lying in the middle of the road. The car must have hit him and killed him. A tear seeped out of the corner of my eye, and I quickly brushed it away. Bex frowned and stopped.

"Are you . . . crying?" she said. I looked at my sister. Years ago, when Mum and Dad first started arguing, we used to sit at the top of the stairs together and listen. She'd put her arm around me and whisper that everything was going to be okay. I really wanted her to do that now.

"No. I'm not crying," I said, frowning at her. She shrugged and kept walking.

There was still one last chance for Monster. One more hope that I was clinging on to. Maybe, just maybe, someone else had rescued him that day and he'd ended up living with my dad. Dad had helped me to save him, in a way. He might not have picked him up out of the road, but he'd driven us to the vet to have Monster's paw looked at. Maybe Monster had survived and was living with him. Okay, it wasn't likely, but I was desperate to believe Monster was okay. I caught up to her again.

"How about your dad? Does he have a dog?"

Bex huffed.

"No. My dad hates dogs!"

I sniffed and wiped my nose.

"He doesn't, actually," I mumbled. "He just says that to annoy Mum."

Bex frowned. "What did you say?" she said.

I didn't look up as I scuffed the floor with my foot. "I'm just saying that sometimes people like dogs more than they think they do, that's all."

Poor Monster. I wanted to sob. I wanted to put my head in my hands and cry. I could feel Bex glaring at me.

"It sounds like a stupid survey to me," she said. "And you're one *really* odd kid."

"Well, you're one *really* bad thief," I said.

Her face dropped.

"What?!" she snarled.

"I saw you stuffing nail polish down your sleeve in that shop!" I said. "Why would you do that? That's not like you *at all*."

She looked angry now. The angriest I'd ever seen her. She got really close to me, and I think if we hadn't been in public, she would have grabbed me by the collar.

"Look, I have no idea who you are or why you think you know anything about me, but if you tell anyone about the nail polish, I'll make sure your life's not worth living. Okay?" she said. Her face was inches from mine, and her makeup was cracking around her nose like pastry on a pie. I took a step back.

"But you don't do things like that," I said, almost shouting.

"You're never in trouble. That's *my* job! You're the good one! You never get detention or set fire to things in school or . . . or steal. You do projects about the Georgians or boring stuff like that—just for *fun!*"

She squinted at me.

"I don't know what you're talking about," she said. "I'm not interested in that stuff."

"Oh yeah?" I said, suddenly remembering the mysterious wooden egg in Reg's cabinet. "I bet you know what *M. Celeste* means, don't you?"

I saw a flicker in my sister's eye, but she didn't say anything.

"Or . . . Amun . . . Amersom . . . Or something like that, anyway. And, um, Earhart. I bet you know what an Earhart is, too, *don't* you?"

She smirked.

"You don't mean *what* an Earhart is, you mean *who*," she said, instantly pressing her lips together. Ha! My sister was in there somewhere after all.

"Who is it, then? Tell me!"

She grimaced at me.

"Haven't you heard of a thing called Google?" she said. We were both quiet for a moment.

"Of course I have! But I don't have a computer at the moment, do I? Or a phone," I said.

She looked me up and down like I was some kind of alien.

"What's your name?" she said.

"Maxwell. Maxwell Bec . . . Just Maxwell," I said.

"Well, Just Maxwell, if you don't have a phone, then that's your problem, not mine," she said, and she carried on walking. I didn't have the energy to follow her and argue anymore, so I turned away and began to walk back to Reg's.

This world stank. My sister was horrible. Really, really horrible. My dad was working in a job that had made him ill, and Charlie Geek was pretending to be someone he wasn't. My stomach churned as I fought back tears.

But far worse than all these things was the realization of what must have happened to my dog. I hadn't been there on that day when he was lying in the middle of the road. I hadn't been there to save him.

I wiped the tears as they began to spill down my cheeks.

My dog, the best thing that had ever happened to me, was gone.

CHAPTER 24
MUM

The next morning I woke with a jump. My heart was thundering in my chest like a rackety old train. Then I remembered why.

I didn't exist anymore.

I'd wished I'd never been born, and for reasons I had no explanation for, it had come true. I looked across at Reg's strange cabinet. I had been standing there just before it had happened. Maybe it had something to do with the strange carved wooden egg? Something weird had happened, and then, in the blink of an eye, I, Maxwell Beckett, had been wiped out of all existence.

And now Monster was dead.

I took some deep breaths like the teachers used to tell me to do when I got angry in class. My heart gradually slowed from a machine-gun fire to a steady thud.

All I needed to do was to work out how the egg had done what it had done, and reverse everything. I'd be un-erased. I would have rescued Monster, and he would still be alive.

Simple.

I could hear Reg puttering around in the kitchen, so I got up and went to the cabinet. I took out the egg and sat on the sofa and gave it a shake. There was a rattling sound inside.

"I wish I existed again," I said, closing my eyes. When I opened them, I looked straight at the mantelpiece, but the picture I'd drawn of Reg wasn't there. I hadn't returned.

Maybe there was more to it than just saying something out loud. I pressed the little knob at the top and it clicked as the egg sprang open again. I took out the handkerchief and had a closer look at the silver button. It was quite fancy and not the kind of button you'd get on clothes today. I put the button on top of the handkerchief and the square of thick fabric and held up the scrap of wool. It was dark gray and looked a bit like an old piece of rag.

"Ah, you've found Amundsen's finger!" said Reg, appearing with two bowls of cornflakes. I dropped the wool and wiped my fingers on my trousers.

"A finger?" I said.

Reg laughed.

"Oh, it's not his actual finger. It's just a piece of his glove. He was someone who . . . he . . . um . . . now I know this one, hold on. Just let me think for a moment."

He put the two bowls onto the coffee table, and his face crumpled as he tried to remember who Amundsen was. I put everything back into the egg and closed it all with a click.

"Don't worry, Reg. There's no need to try and remember," I said, reaching for my cornflakes. "Do you have a laptop I could borrow?"

Reg picked up his bowl of cornflakes and looked at me blankly.

"I don't think I've got one of those, young, um . . . um . . ."

He was struggling to remember my name. I munched on a big spoonful of cereal.

"Thanks for breakfast, Reg. My parents said you'd be a great person to stay with while they were away. Dad said, 'Oh, Maxwell, you'll have a lovely time with Reg.' And he was right."

I gave him a smile. I was quite pleased that I'd managed to tell him my name again without him feeling uncomfortable. He smiled back at me.

"Maxwell! Of course. Maxwell. Right you are." He scraped his spoon around the bowl, and we both ate our breakfasts in silence.

There was something I really wanted to do today. I wanted to see my mum. I wasn't going to talk to her or freak her out or anything, but maybe I could follow her home and double-check that there was no sign of Monster. My sister was so horrible, I didn't quite trust that she wasn't lying when she said she didn't have a dog.

My best hope of seeing Mum was to go to where she worked— assuming she still worked there—and wait outside until she finished her shift at two p.m.

"Reg?" I asked. "Can I look through your cabinet this morning?"

Reg looked at me and smiled.

"Of course you can!" he said. "There are some wonderful things in there. Truly wonderful."

"Do you know anything about the wooden egg?" I asked. "The one that opens up with all the things inside? You said your grandfather won it in Vietnam."

Reg chewed on the inside of his cheek as he thought about it. Then he shrugged. It didn't look like he could remember any more than that.

After we finished breakfast, Reg went off to the kitchen to do the washing up while I looked through the shelves of the cabinet. From what I could tell, most of it was junk. There were a few books on the bottom shelf, and one of the titles caught my eye: *The Mary Celeste Mystery*. That was one of the names carved on the inside of the egg, I was sure of it! I took the egg out of the cabinet and sat on the floor with the book beside me. I pressed the top and opened it up, then took all the things out. Then I looked closely at the engraved names again.

M. Celeste.

There it was. The name matched the book!

There was a painting of a ship on the cover—an old-fashioned kind with big, billowing sails. I turned the book over and read the blurb on the back:

In 1872 the merchant vessel the *Mary Celeste* was discovered drifting across the Atlantic Ocean. It was completely deserted. The ship wasn't damaged and there were no signs of a fight. The lifeboat was missing, but the provisions were still stored in the cupboards. The last entry in her log had been made ten days earlier. What happened is a complete mystery . . .

I felt the hairs at the back of my neck go all electric-y. Where had everybody gone? Had they all just jumped off the ship? Had something taken them?

I looked at the little pile of things that were inside the egg— the button, the woolen "finger," the handkerchief, and the piece of fabric. I studied each one, then held the fabric against the picture of the ship. My tummy turned over and my arms tingled. The dirty-white cloth in my hand looked very similar to the big, curling sails on the ship. Was I holding a piece of the *Mary Celeste*?

I spent the rest of the morning looking through the book, but it didn't give any answers to what had happened. The last chapter finished with the line: *The disappearance of the crew on the* Mary Celeste *is a mystery that will never be solved* . . . Was I going to end up like that? Was I going to be an unsolvable mystery? I shut the book and quickly put it away. It gave me the shivers.

We had baked beans on toast for lunch, and then it was almost time to try and see Mum. I told Reg that I had to go out and run some errands but I wouldn't be long.

———

Mum works in a clinic on the edge of town. She's a phlebotomist, which sounds like something to do with bottoms, but it actually means she takes people's blood.

It was a long way to the clinic, but the walk gave me a chance to think. I felt nervous. What if she wasn't there? I couldn't see her working anywhere else, because she absolutely loved her job, but then Dad wasn't doing his gardening anymore, so maybe things were different for her, too.

Mum had had this job for as long as I could remember. When I was really little, she bought me a toy medical kit and taught me how to take a blood test. Not a real one; the syringe I used was just made of chunky plastic without a needle or anything. Mum would pretend to be the patient and I would be the phlebotomist. She would sit on one of our dining chairs in the middle of the kitchen, and I'd ask her to confirm her name, address, and date of birth while I stared at a little notepad. I was too young to read or write, so I just nodded and scribbled on the paper. I'd then ask Mum to roll up her sleeve and hold out her arm. I pretended to look for a vein, but she always had a bright greeny-blue one right there that I tapped with my fingertip. I wrapped a bandage above her elbow (which you did to make the vein stand out better), then wiped her arm with a piece of tissue like I was making it clean. I got my syringe ready.

"Sharp scratch coming, Mum. I mean, Mrs. Beckett," I said, and Mum giggled.

I pretended to take the blood, and then I asked her to press down on a cotton ball on the inside of her elbow, before putting a real Band-Aid on the invisible spot. Putting the Band-Aid on was my favorite bit.

"What a gentle, professional phlebotomist you are," said Mum.

"I'm the best bottom-ist ever!" I'd say, which would make Mum really laugh. I used to love that time with her, playing pretend games like that. I wished I could go back and do it all again.

The clinic was farther than I remembered, and I had to jog for the last five minutes to make sure I was there by two p.m. I got to the door just as Mum appeared in the foyer area. I smiled. She looked exactly the same! She tucked her short brown hair behind one ear as she swung her bag onto her shoulder and stopped to say something to a man sitting at the reception desk. They both laughed and then she came out of the door, brushing right past me. I watched as she put her hands into her coat pockets and walked through the parking lot to the road. I quickly followed.

It was so nice to see my mum that I started to wonder if there was a way I could talk to her. Maybe I could just pretend I knew her. Or ask her something about the clinic. I sped up a little with a big smile on my face, but then I saw Mum wave at a man standing by the parking lot entrance. He wiggled his fingers back at her. I slowed down again. I'd never seen that man before. He was wearing a gray sweater, with a puffy green vest over it. He grinned at my mum, and then something terrible happened. Something that made me sick to my stomach. The man held out his arms and Mum skipped toward him, and he folded his arms around her in a great big hug. Mum had her face pressed against his chest, and then, as if it couldn't get worse, she turned her face toward his and they kissed.

And it wasn't a "hello" kiss, either.

It was a proper kiss on the lips.

And it went on for ages.

"W-what are you doing, Mum?" I said under my breath.

When they'd stopped kissing, the man stood back and smiled at her like she was the best thing he'd ever seen in the whole wide world. She put her arm in his and they walked down the road toward town.

I wanted to throw up.

She had a *boyfriend*? My *mum*? I couldn't believe it. Okay, so Mum and Dad hadn't been happy for a while, and they lived as separately as they could in our house, but I'd never known either of them to go out with anyone else. *Ever.*

I was just a few paces behind them, but it was hard to keep my distance because they were walking *really* slowly. It was like they weren't in a rush to be anywhere. Mum said something, and the man laughed and kissed her on the top of her head as she pressed the side of her face against his big arm.

"Oh please," I groaned, a little too loudly. The man looked over his shoulder and frowned, and then my mum turned, too. She looked me right in the eyes and smiled. I smiled back. She recognized me! I was about to say hello, but she turned away and they carried on walking. My heart sank. She didn't know me at all. I was just some kid who happened to be going the same way. I was nobody to her.

They got to the main street and paused outside a café, looking at the menu as I walked past.

My stomach was in knots as I stopped at a thrift store next to the café. I pretended to look in the window while stealing glances at Mum and the man. They chose some seats under an orange heater and sat down, holding hands across the table. I hadn't seen her look that happy in years, and I didn't like it. Not that she was happy, but the reason why. It was that man, in his stupid puffy vest that made him look like he had a life jacket on. I could hear them discussing what they were going to order. The man chose the vegan lasagna and Mum picked the tofu stir-fry. She'd have never chosen a tofu stir-fry with Dad; she'd have had a burger or something.

I was just thinking that I couldn't really stand there for much longer when Mum went inside the café to order. The man took his cell phone out of his vest pocket and began scrolling through it. Before I thought about it too much, I walked toward him and stood by his chair. It took him a moment to realize I was there.

"Ah, my partner's just gone inside to order, actually," he said, smiling at me. I smirked. He actually thought I worked here! A twelve-year-old working in a café on a school day?! That's how *stupid* he was. What an idiot!

"Your girlfriend seems nice," I blurted out. I could see my mum inside, standing in a line at the till.

"Um. Yeah, she is," said the man, looking at me strangely. "Do we know you?"

I snorted.

"No. *We* don't know me at all," I said, realizing it didn't really make sense, but I knew what I meant.

The man nodded, then sort of shrugged in a "So what do you want, then?" kind of way.

"You do know she killed a hedgehog once, don't you?"

The man opened his mouth and closed it again.

"She ran over it," I said. "It went right under her wheel."

"A hedgehog?" he asked.

"Yes," I said. "It exploded like a balloon right across the road. Like this . . . BANG!" The man flinched as I slammed my hands together.

"I thought you should know. What with you not eating animals and all that," I said.

"I see," he said. "And did she eat the hedgehog? After she'd killed it?"

I pulled a face.

"No, of course not," I said. He was studying my face like teachers do sometimes when they're trying to be cleverer than you are.

"Well, these things happen. I'm sure most people have accidentally killed something when driving," he said. He was right.

Mum had run over the hedgehog by mistake and had come home crying about it.

"I'm sorry, but why are you telling me this?" he said, sitting forward in his chair. I looked inside the café and Mum was at the counter, being served. I had to be quick.

"I just wanted to warn you about her," I said, nodding toward the café. "Her kids are a nightmare. Her eldest daughter is a handful. She'll probably end up in jail before long. And her youngest, well, he's just out of control. Did she tell you he decapitated a flamingo once? He took its head right off with a brick."

I didn't mention that the flamingo had been made of plastic. The man looked at me and smiled.

"Are you okay?" he said kindly. "Is there someone you'd like me to call?"

I opened my mouth to say something else when the door of the café opened and my mum walked right toward us.

"Oh, hello. Are you one of Dan's players?" she said, sitting beside the man and taking his hand.

"Players?" I croaked.

"On his basketball team? The Super Dans?" she said, looking at me and then back at Super Dan. I shook my head.

"I think there's been some kind of mix-up here," said Super Dan, giving me a big, cheesy smile. "This young man has gotten us confused with someone else, I think. Amanda has just the one child, you see. There's no crazy boy decapitating flamingos in our house," he said, laughing. *They lived together?!* His eyes crinkled at the edges when he smiled.

"You know, I'm always looking for new players for the Super

Dans, if you're interested in giving basketball a try! I take on all abilities. Get your parents to give the sports center a call."

My mum let out a giggle.

"Oh, Dan, not everyone wants to play basketball, you know!" she said. She looked at me. "He's *always* scouting for players!"

"I just like to see kids running around and enjoying themselves, that's all," he said.

They stared into each other's eyes and then pecked each other on the lips.

I nearly threw up right there and then.

"Anyway," I shouted, slapping my hands on the table so they both jumped. "Like I was saying, Dan, you should have a serious think about, you know . . . the hedgehog thing . . . what with you being vegan and all."

I tapped the side of my head as Dan's jaw dropped.

I jiggled around, not quite knowing the best way to say it, so I just came out with it.

"Do you have a dog?" I said, directly to Mum. "A fat beagle with bad breath?"

Super Dan laughed as he reached over and held Mum's hand.

"No. We don't have a dog," he said. "Are you sure there's not someone we could call?" He said it all calmly like I was some kind of crazy person.

"No," I said. "No phone call, thank you."

And then I turned and ran away.

CHAPTER 25
FLOWERS

Poor Monster. He really wasn't anywhere. He'd gone, and there wasn't anything I could do to bring him back. And Mum had seemed so happy with Super Dan it made me feel really sad for Dad. I wanted to see him and check that he was okay. I could also ask him if he had a beagle, not that I was holding out much hope now. I walked around the town for hours, keeping warm by hiding at the back of the library until, eventually, it was getting to the time when Dad would be heading home from work. I sat on the bench outside the station and waited.

Every twenty minutes or so, there was a surge of people as a train arrived from London. It was just as it had been the other morning when Dad had dropped his phone, but this time the crowds were walking in the other direction and not as quickly.

After another rush of people, a lone man came slowly through the ticket barriers and out onto the street.

It was Dad.

His cheeks were red and he had deep gray bags under his eyes. His forehead was creased, and he looked absolutely awful. I hated seeing him like that, and my mind whirled as I tried to think of something I could say to help him. I looked along the street, and then I had an idea. I ran past Dad and stopped in front of a florist's. It was closed, but that didn't matter—I didn't need to go in. My dad got closer and closer and then I jumped out toward him.

"Excuse me. I wonder if you could help me with something?"

My dad frowned at me and looked around.

"Um. Okay," he said cautiously. He looked even worse close up—just like he had when he'd stopped going to work all those years ago.

"It's my mum's birthday soon, and I want to buy her some flowers. Do you know what that flower is, right there?"

I pointed to a photograph of a red flower that was in the florist's window. My dad took a step closer and looked at the picture.

"Er . . . yeah, it's a rose."

"Ah . . . right. And what about that pink one there?" I said, pointing to a vase in the window. My dad looked at me like I was losing the plot. "She likes pink, you see, so I want to make sure I get the right kind."

Dad huffed, then looked in the window.

"That's a dahlia," he said.

"A dahlia! Brilliant. Wow, you really do know a lot about plants and stuff, don't you?"

My dad shrugged.

"No, not really. They're quite common. Well, good luck with your mum's birthday."

He walked on, and I stumbled along beside him.

"I'd say working with plants must be quite relaxing, wouldn't you? I mean, who would choose to work in a stuffy office when you could be outside in the fresh air?"

My dad took a sideways look at me, then stopped.

"Hang on. Aren't you that kid who picked my phone up for

me the other morning? Outside the station?" I opened my mouth and shut it again.

"Um . . . no? I don't think so. I don't remember that, anyway. That must have been someone else."

He shook his head, then turned and carried on. I felt my stomach knot. I followed a few paces behind him. When Dad had been off sick from his stressful job and we'd chatted in the garden, I was sure that something I had said had made him decide to quit his job and go back to college. Maybe I could try again. I caught up to him.

"You know, I was just thinking of something someone told me once," I said. "Something about work."

"Oh yeah, what was that, then?" he said, not looking at me. I was irritating him now, I could tell.

"What this person said was: Why do a job that you don't like very much?" I said it all dramatically.

Dad stopped again and faced me. He laughed a bit, but it wasn't a nice laugh. It was a sarcastic one.

"Yeah, well, real life doesn't work like that, I'm afraid."

"But it does! I know this man . . . He's a bit like you, actually. And he had a job that he hated, and it was so stressful that it . . . it made him ill. And he carried a brick around in his pocket, but he didn't always notice it was there . . . or something like that . . . but then . . . then he decided that it wasn't worth all the misery and he quit. He became a gardener. Maybe you could do that. Seeing as you like flowers and stuff."

My dad smiled.

"Well, that's great. Good luck to him. But I've got rent and bills to pay and . . . sometimes life just doesn't work in your favor, you know?"

He walked away, his head hanging low. This time I didn't follow him. I just watched as he disappeared into the distance, getting smaller and smaller and smaller.

I didn't get it. I had said exactly the same thing to my dad, but this time he hadn't even thought about it at all. Why hadn't it worked? And I didn't get a chance to ask him about Monster.

I had to find a way back to my proper life, where things were normal, but first I had to work out how I'd been erased. It had something to do with that egg in Reg's cabinet, I was sure of it.

As I walked, I spotted two girls outside a shop. One of them had a high ponytail and I realized it was Bex. She had her arms folded and was facing another girl. It was Claudia, her worst enemy in the world. I got closer so that I could hear what was going on.

"I can't go back in there," my sister said. "The guy has seen me too many times. He's getting suspicious! *You've* got to do it."

Claudia flicked her hair from one shoulder to the other.

"Don't be stupid," she said. "That's what *you're* for. I'm not getting caught."

Claudia took a step closer to my sister so her face was just inches away from hers and then said something through gritted teeth that I couldn't hear. Bex kept her head down, and then Claudia strutted off down the sidewalk.

My sister turned and spotted me.

"What are *you* doing here?" she spat. "Are you following me again?"

I shook my head.

"I—I wanted to ask you something. About history. You knew about someone called Armun . . . Amund-thingy . . . I need to find out who he was."

Bex gave me a look, then rolled her eyes.

"So what if I do? Don't you have someone else to ask?"

I thought about it for a bit and shook my head.

"Not really, no," I said.

She suddenly started to chew some gum that she must have had stuffed in the corner of her mouth. Her face turned from a grimace into a smile.

"Look. I tell you what. If you do something for me, then I'll tell you what that means, okay?"

I stared as her jaw went up and down.

"What do I have to do?" I asked.

Bex looked around her.

"I want you to get a new phone case from the shop on the main street. The one that does repairs. Do you know it?"

I nodded. It was a tiny shop in between a pharmacy and a clothes shop.

"Go in there tomorrow, get the case for me, and then I'll tell you who Amundsen was."

She got her phone out of her pocket and swiped at the screen. She turned it toward me and showed me an image of a phone case with a Union Jack design on the back.

"It's got to be *exactly* that one or the deal is off. Okay?"

I stared at the picture.

"Obviously it goes without saying that if you get caught, then it's totally your problem. And if you mention any of this to anyone, then you'll live to regret it. Meet me at the town library during lunch at twelve thirty. Okay?"

I nodded again, and she walked away. I couldn't believe my sister was blackmailing me into stealing in return for telling me something about history. It was bonkers.

I fought back tears as I began to walk slowly toward Reg's house. I didn't want to be in this world anymore. I wanted to be back home, where my sister was a nerd who would never steal anything in her life. I wanted my dad back doing the job he loved and to see my mum without a stupid boyfriend. I wanted to see my best friend, Charlie, being his usual nerdy self again. But, most of all, I wanted my dog. I wanted Monster to be alive again so I could give him the biggest hug ever.

I'd had enough of being erased.

I wanted to exist again.

CHAPTER 26
TEARS

When I got to Reg's, I let myself in through the kitchen. The TV was on, but the old man was asleep. His head was tipped back and he had his mouth open. His throat rattled as he snored.

I stood in front of the old cabinet. The weird wooden egg was on its side where I'd left it. I had a gut feeling it was somehow responsible for what had happened to me. Or maybe it was the old globe dotted with strange, tiny holes? I picked it up and stared at it. I remembered seeing this when I was really angry after the Hundredth Anniversary Celebration. Could the globe have erased me somehow? I held it in my hands and turned it around slowly.

"I want . . . I want to exist again," I whispered, feeling like a bit of an idiot.

I held the globe for a moment, then shook it up and down three times. I'm not sure why I did that, but I felt like I had to do something else. I took a deep breath, then put the globe back on the shelf.

I could feel something fizzing in my stomach, the kind of fizzing I got on Christmas morning. Maybe that meant it had worked?!

I left Reg snoring and ran out of the kitchen door. I skipped down the pathway and then sprinted toward my house. As I ran, I planned exactly what I was going to do when I got home. First,

I was going to make a big fuss over Monster, and then I'd give Mum and Dad a big kiss. I'd even give Bex a hug. It would be nice to see her looking like her usual self again. I'd then run over to see Charlie and see if he wanted to hang out or something. It was getting late now, though, so I didn't expect he could, but I'd still like to see him. But as I turned the corner onto my street, I saw that there was a strange red car parked on our driveway.

And it got worse.

The gate was still there.

The gate that I'd busted all those years ago was still in its place, unbroken. I walked up the path and stared in through the living room window. I could hear some music playing. The man I'd seen through the patio door was standing, pouring a glass of red wine for another man in a white shirt and jeans. The man in the white shirt said something, and they both tipped their heads back and laughed.

I turned away before I was spotted.

It hadn't worked. There were strangers living in my house. My family was all wrong. And Monster. Well, I couldn't bear to think about what might have happened to my dog.

———

When I got back to the bungalow, Reg was in the kitchen. I explained who I was, and while he listened he got a jar out of the cupboard.

"Can I interest you in a cocoa, Maxwell?" he said, and I nodded. I watched him making our drinks.

"Reg, do you remember I asked you what you'd do if you didn't exist in the world anymore? If you'd been erased from your life but everyone was still here?"

Reg looked blank, but I carried on.

"Well, I know it sounds mad, but . . . but I think it might have happened to me."

The old man nodded as he passed me my drink. We went and sat in the living room.

"I think it happened when I came here after I messed up at the Hundredth Anniversary Celebration. After I'd shut off the electricity. I didn't mean to be erased. Not really. And now . . . and now I want to go back. I want to go back to see my family and to tell Charlie Geek that he's my best friend in the whole world. And I want to see my dog again. I want Monster to be alive."

I could feel the tears coming, so I put my drink down, and then I began to sob.

"Oh dear," said Reg. "Oh dear, dear, dearie me."

I covered my face with my hands and felt the sofa sag as he sat down beside me. An old blue-checked handkerchief appeared under my nose, and I took it and used it to wipe my eyes.

"I don't know what to do, Reg. I think it was something in the cabinet. I think something in there made it happen. I think it's that egg. Something magical happened, and I need . . . I need to undo it. Do you have any idea what it could be?"

"Something in my cabinet?" he chuckled. "I don't think that's possible, do you?"

I shrugged at him.

"I don't know, Reg. I just know that I need to get home. I'm worried that if I don't exist, then my dog is dead. I *want* to go home."

I cried some more, and he patted me slowly on the back.

"There, there. We'll have a think about what to do. Let old Reg have a little think and we'll come up with a plan, okay? Together we'll work out what to do. Don't you worry."

He patted me three more times and then stopped and stood up.

"I know what we could do!" he said brightly. I looked up at him.

"Yes?" I said.

Reg gave me a big, wide smile.

"Let's have a nice piece of Victoria sponge cake. How about that for a plan?"

I opened my mouth and closed it. I wanted to cry again, but I swallowed the tears away.

"That'll be great. Thank you . . . thank you, Reg," I said, and as he made his way to the kitchen, I dabbed the handkerchief on my eyes.

CHAPTER 27

SHOP

I could see Monster lying in the middle of the road. He had his back to me, and as I got closer, he lifted up his head. His tail thumped slowly onto the hot tarmac, his tongue dangling out of the side of his mouth like he was grinning.

"Monster? Are you hurt?" I said. I heard an engine rev and looked along the street. A car was coming and it was getting faster. I looked back at Monster, who was still staring at me, his tail thump, thump, thumping onto the ground. The car was heading straight for him. If he didn't move out of the way, he'd be hit!

I went to step off the curb, but my feet wouldn't move. I looked down at my legs and tried to lift them, but they were completely stuck. It was as if my shoes had been superglued to the pavement.

"Monster! You've got to get out of the way! You've got to get up!" I shouted, trying desperately to move.

I looked at the car speeding toward my dog. Through the window I could see the driver on his phone, looking into his rearview mirror.

"Monster! NO!!!!" I screamed. The car made a horrendous *sccrreeeechhh* and I woke up.

My heart banged against my ribs as I stared at Reg's living room ceiling. It was a dream. But it had felt so real. Not being able to get off the curb and save Monster was agonizing. It was exactly how I was feeling now, trapped in this world where my dog was dead because I didn't exist. I *had* to get home. I got up, went to the kitchen, and put the kettle on. I felt queasy when I thought about what faced me today. Today there would be no more "nice Maxwell." Today I was going to be a shoplifter.

Reg spent all morning chatting about this and that, but I wasn't really listening. All I could think about was how I was going to steal the phone case and how I was going to turn the world back to how it was before.

I headed to the main street at the last possible moment, and when I got to the Fone Place, my stomach was churning even more. It was a tiny shop, about half the size of Reg's living room, and the man who owned it was sitting at the back, fiddling with the phones. I'd been in there once with Mum. The speaker on her phone had stopped working, and we watched as the man took it apart and removed a huge piece of fluff. He'd said there was no charge, so I knew he was a nice man, and I really didn't want to steal anything from him. I hung around outside, pretending to look at the ads in his window, and then I couldn't leave it any longer. The doorbell pinged as I went in, and the man looked up over his glasses.

"Afternoon," he said. "Can I help?"

I stuck my hands in my pockets and smiled.

"I'm just looking, thanks," I said. He raised his eyebrows a bit and then he looked back down at what he was doing.

The shop was so tiny that "just looking" would take approximately eight seconds. I walked straight to the stand of phone cases and slowly turned it around, trying to find the Union Jack one.

There was one left, hanging on a hook right at the top. I reached up and took it down. It was the right case in the right size and exactly the one I was after. I glanced over at the man, who was still looking down at what he was doing. I was just going to slip the case into my jacket when the shop man suddenly started talking.

"Speakers are amazing, aren't they?" he said.

I froze.

"I'm sorry?" I said.

"Speakers. I mean . . . take this tiny thing here . . ." He held up a sliver of silver between the points of a pair of tweezers. "This piece of mesh is a gateway to a world of discovery."

I blinked at him.

"Through this tiny square you can choose to listen to the cleverest scientists in the world discussing the mysteries of the universe, or maybe the most beautiful piece of classical music ever created, or perhaps a cricket match being played on the other side of the world. Technology is amazing when you think about it, isn't it?"

"I s'pose so," I said, still holding the Union Jack case in my hand.

"Take my wife, for example. She drives a truck and she always has one of those audiobooks on, playing in her cab. She listens to those stories for hours and hours. She loves it! She's read hundreds of books *without* actually reading any of them! Brilliant!"

He was grinning at me, waiting for me to say something.

"My friend listens to the sun," I said. The man's grin fixed on his face. Why was I telling him this? I still had the phone case in my hand. I couldn't exactly steal it now, could I?

"The Sun?" said the man. "What is that, a new band or something?"

"No, the actual sun. He found some recordings on the Internet. It was the sound the sun's magnetic field makes . . . or something like that anyway. Someone made a recording of it."

The man stared at me.

"That is incredible. See what I mean? See what I mean?" he repeated, his eyes wide. "How incredible is that? The sound of a burning star. Amazing . . . just amazing . . ."

He stared off into the distance, and I took the chance to step to one side, pretending I was looking at some reconditioned phones in a cabinet. I slipped the phone case into the waistband of my jeans, pulling my jacket down to hide it from view.

"Did you know that in the nineteenth century they could make music boxes so tiny they could fit inside a necklace pendant? Isn't that fascinating?"

I stared at him and swallowed. A music box? Wasn't that what Reg had called the wooden egg? My mind raced. The more I thought about it, the more I was sure he'd called it a music box. And there had been some noises coming from the box just before I'd been erased. Some kind of plinky noises that had reminded me of my sister's old jewelry box. But then I'd pulled everything out of the cabinet when I was trying to look for Reg's portrait. Had I broken the egg? It had definitely been lying on the floor, I was certain of that.

"Anyway, are you looking to buy a new phone case?" said the shopkeeper. "What size are you after?"

I could feel my cheeks beginning to burn. The man watched me closely.

"Oh, I've . . . I've changed my mind," I said, blinking back at him.

He opened his mouth to say something else when I quickly turned around and ran.

CHAPTER 28

LIBRARY

The library assistant looked up at me from her desk when I walked in, and then she turned back to her computer. I walked around the library and found Bex in the history section. She was sitting at a table with her head hanging over a book. When she saw me, she quickly closed it.

"You got it?" she whispered. I took the phone case out from my jacket and slid it across the table as I sat down. Her face seemed to relax. Claudia clearly had some kind of hold over her. The whole thing stank.

"Okay, now it's time for your side of the bargain. Tell me what you know about Amun-whatsit," I said.

She stared at me again and then checked around before she began.

"Right. Listen up and concentrate 'cause I'm only going to say this once."

I nodded.

"Roald Amundsen was a Norwegian explorer. In 1911, he led an expedition team to try and be the first people to reach the South Pole. His team did it—they got there first. It was an incredible achievement."

Now that she said it, I kind of remembered seeing something about that on TV once. There had been a black-and-white photograph of some men in the snow wearing thick fur clothing. I remember wondering if the fur clothes had been warm enough. Maybe that piece of woolen fabric had something to do with it.

"Did something happen to Amundsen? At the South Pole?" I asked, swallowing.

"No. They returned from the Pole okay, but a few years later Amundsen was part of a rescue team that went out to the Arctic to help try and find a missing airship."

She paused, but I already had a feeling that this wasn't going to end well.

"Amundsen's plane never made it," she said. "He and the crew were never found."

I shuddered.

"Just like the *Mary Celeste*," I said. "Another disappearance."

Bex narrowed her eyes at me.

"You know about the ghost ship, then?" she said, and I nodded.

"The ship was found adrift in the ocean, and all the crew members were missing," I said. "No one knows what happened to them. It's a mystery that will never be solved."

Bex popped a little bubble in her gum.

"I read about it in a book," I added.

She grinned at me.

"See? You didn't need a phone or computer after all!" she said.

My mind was buzzing. That was two disappearances connected to the egg: the *Mary Celeste* and Roald Amundsen, the Arctic explorer.

"Why all the questions?" she asked.

I was trying to think of a reason for asking, but I decided to just tell the truth. Part of it, anyway.

"I've got a friend who has a collection of old things, but he's not sure what they are. I said I'd try and find out for him."

"What sort of things?" she said, shuffling in her seat.

"Um, well, there's a little square of thick fabric. I think that's a piece of sail from the *Mary Celeste*," I said.

Bex snorted.

"You have *got* to be kidding me."

I smiled at her shocked face.

"No! It's all there in a cabinet in his living room," I said proudly. "There's a finger from a glove that I think might have belonged to Amundsen and, um . . . someone's handkerchief, but I can't remember their name. And a silver button belonging to someone else."

She stared at me for a bit.

"Do you think I could come and see them? I might be able to tell you what they are."

I grinned.

"Yes! Come after school. You'll love it! There's all sorts of old stuff in there, and I bet you'll know what everything is because you know so much about history and . . ."

Her face fell and she looked at me weirdly.

"I mean . . . you look like someone who would know a lot about history."

She stood up and put her bag over her shoulder.

"Look, don't tell anyone about this, will you?"

"What, the phone case?" I said.

"Well, obviously that!" she said, doing her famous eye roll

again. "But also the bit about me being in here, in the library. Keep that to yourself, all right?"

I realized that, for this version of Bex, being seen in a library would be incredibly embarrassing. I shrugged and gave her Reg's address. As she left to go back to school, I smiled to myself. My sister was going to help me get back home!

CHAPTER 29
CABINET

When I got back to the bungalow, the first thing I did was check the egg again. I looked at the little wooden knob on the top. I remembered now! Before I'd been erased, I'd wound the little knob like a watch. But when I tried again, it just spun around and around. There were no little noises, no notes. I gave it a shake and it rattled like something was loose inside. I opened it up, and then I noticed that in the middle of the egg was a small boxed area. That must be where the workings that played the music were. The man in the phone shop had said that they could make music boxes really small. I closed the egg and went to the window to wait for Bex. My sister had a super brain. She'd definitely work out how I could get home, I was sure of it. I wasn't planning on telling her who I was or what had happened; I was just hoping she'd come up with something to explain what was going on.

I spent the rest of the afternoon helping Reg with his chores and, every now and then, checking out the window for any sign of my sister. It wasn't long before I saw her high ponytail appear around the corner. I went to the side door and waved at her to come that way. She looked fed up, but I guessed that was probably because she'd had to stay behind at school again.

Reg was in the kitchen boiling some water in a saucepan on the stove. There was a box of pasta on the side and two bowls.

"Ah, Maxwell! I'm just getting dinner on. Who's your friend?" he said.

"This is Bex. She's my . . . she's my . . . she's Bex."

Bex glared at me. She really didn't look very happy at all.

"Are you staying for dinner, Bex? It's pasta."

She ignored him and turned to me.

"Are we going to look at this cabinet, then, or what?"

Luckily Reg didn't appear to notice how rude she was being.

"Can I show Bex some of the things in your cabinet, Reg? She's really interested in history."

I heard Bex's huff, but I didn't look at her. Reg waved a hand at us.

"Of course! There are some real precious treasures in there, Bex. Be very careful, though. Put everything back *exactly* where you found it, won't you? Everything has a place."

He turned away and fiddled with the box of pasta, and Bex and I made our way to the living room.

"Ta-da!" I said, extending my hand toward the cabinet. "Look at it! I bet you can't wait to have a look through all that, can you?" Bex sniffed and folded her arms like she really wasn't interested, but I saw her eyes quickly scanning all the shelves. I opened the glass doors, and Bex reached for the dark brown globe.

"This looks really old," said Bex.

"I wonder what the little holes mean," I said, watching her run her fingers across the dots over Africa.

"I reckon the owner made punctures for all the places they visited," she said.

I grinned at her. She'd solved a puzzle already! But Bex just frowned at me and shoved the globe into my chest.

"Where's the piece of sail, then?" she said. She really wasn't in a good mood at all.

I picked up the wooden egg and carefully opened it, revealing the items inside.

"It's a music box. The workings are in the bottom, I think. But it's broken." I didn't tell her it was because I had pulled everything out of the cabinet in a rage.

"Each of the four sides has something written on it. See?" I said.

Bex took a step closer and peered inside, and I passed the egg to her.

"*M. Celeste,*" she said quietly, pointing to the engraved words. I took the piece of sail out of the middle and gave it to her. Bex stuck out her bottom lip as she held the piece of fabric in between her fingers.

"It's definitely too thick to be clothing or some kind of sheeting," she said, holding it up to the light. "And it looks really old. The material looks strong. It could be a part of a sail, I guess."

Her eyes twinkled a little, and I smiled at her. She put it down and reached for the piece of glove, and then she looked at the engraved names inside the egg again.

"*Amundsen,*" she read.

"I think that might be part of his glove?" I said. I saw Bex's throat go up and down as she swallowed.

I picked up the handkerchief and passed it to Bex. She held it to the light and looked at the initials *A. E.* embroidered in the corner, and then she looked back at the words written inside the egg.

"Earhart," she said, tracing the engraving. I noticed her hands were trembling.

"Did this . . ." she said, her voice cracking a little. "Did this really belong to Amelia Earhart?" She looked at me, but I just shrugged.

"I dunno," I said. "Who was she?"

"She . . . she was incredible," said Bex, clearing her throat. "Amelia Earhart was an American aviator and the first woman to fly solo across the Atlantic. A real adventurer! But in 1937 she tried to fly around the world and she disappeared over the Pacific Ocean."

The room went silent.

"What happened to her?" I whispered.

Bex held the handkerchief close to her face, studying every stitch.

"No one knows. It's assumed she crashed into the sea, but they never found her or the plane."

I could feel my skin prickle with goose bumps. Bex stroked the handkerchief, then carefully folded it up.

"The final name carved on the egg is *Louis Le Prince.* Who was he?" I asked.

Bex picked up the little silver button.

"I've no idea," she said, studying it closely. "But I'm guessing that this is his button. It looks like it's made of real silver, too."

Reg appeared from behind the kitchen door, and Bex jumped a little.

"Pasta's ready, Maxwell," he said, clapping his hands together. "Would your friend like some, too?"

Bex shook her head. Reg went back to the kitchen again, and I could hear him getting the cutlery out of the drawer.

"I gotta go," she said quickly, shoving the egg toward me.

"Don't you want to look through the other stuff?" I said. "There's probably loads in here that you'll know about."

She looked at the cabinet and her nose curled upward.

"It's just a bunch of worthless junk, Maxwell," she said. "There's nothing of interest in here."

I couldn't believe it.

"What? But you were really excited about it a minute ago. You were shaking when you looked at Amelia Earhart's handkerchief! I saw you!"

Bex scowled at me.

"No, I wasn't! Think about it, Maxwell. If these things were real, why would they be stuffed in a cabinet in an old guy's bungalow, eh? It's just a pile of rubbish."

My heart sank. I really thought that she'd explain something that would help me find my way back home.

"But these are all things you love and care about!" I said. "This is history! 'History Ain't Dead'—remember? You always say that. You've even got it on a T-shirt!"

Bex looked at me with disgust in her eyes.

"I've never said that before in my life," she said. She put her schoolbag onto her shoulder and walked out of the kitchen without another word.

CHAPTER 30
STEP

I spent the night thinking over what Bex had said about the cabinet being full of rubbish. Maybe she was right. But so far I'd discovered three things that had something to do with a disappearance: Amundsen's glove finger, the *Mary Celeste* sail, and Amelia Earhart's handkerchief. And they were all inside the egg. Surely that wasn't a coincidence. That egg definitely had something to do with me being erased.

The next morning I decided that Charlie Geek was my next best hope to help me get out of this mess. Like my sister, he was smart and knew about loads of stuff. Especially science. There must be something scientific behind what had happened. Maybe he could get the music box working again. And this time I was going to tell the truth—I was going to tell him exactly what had happened to me. I'd tell him that I'd been erased. Plus, I needed to borrow some new clothes because these ones were really starting to stink.

I didn't want to risk being seen at school again, so I decided to wait for Charlie at his house. His mum worked full-time, so there wouldn't be anyone around asking awkward questions. I sat on their front step and stared at the scruffy garden while I waited for him to get home from school.

Charlie and his mum used the front garden, and the people upstairs in the duplex used the back. When we were seven, I got the idea that we could make a super-deluxe "Dirt-Track Mountain" on an empty flower bed. We asked his mum, and she said she didn't mind what we did, as long as we cleared up any mess. We moved buckets of earth from one side of the garden to the flower bed and piled it up into a great big mound. We used fat sticks to scrape out a circular track, and Charlie stuck a big leaf at the top that he said was the starting post. We then pushed our toy cars along the track while making *brrrrrrr* and *nerrrrrr* noises. Charlie knew all the makes and models of the cars, and he always let me have the fastest, coolest one. Although actually, I probably made him give it to me. I probably made him do a lot of things that he didn't want to do. I was that kind of "friend" to him. Not a good one.

After we'd played with Dirt-Track Mountain a few times, we lost interest in it, but the big mound of earth stayed there, piled high in the corner. Over the years, the "mountain" became covered with weeds.

I looked at the same corner of the garden and rubbed the side of my face. The flower bed where we'd piled tons of earth was completely flat. It wasn't such a shock to me anymore now. It was just a fact: I hadn't existed to have had the idea for Dirt-Track Mountain in the first place, so it had never been made. The memories I had in my head were mine and mine only. I had a past that no one else had shared. Nobody at all. The thought of that made me feel lonely. Very lonely.

I gave a deep sigh, and when I looked up, Charlie Geek was walking right toward me.

"What are *you* doing here?" he said. His hair was still spiked up and his school tie was hanging around his neck, undone.

I jumped up and brushed off the back of my jeans.

"Charlie! Good to see you, again!" I said, trying to sound friendly. I grinned at him, but he just scowled.

"Look, I know you're a bit freaked about why I keep turning up . . . but I need your help. Can I explain?" I said.

Charlie stared back, his eyes narrowing to little slits.

"No," he said. He rummaged around in his bag, took out his door key, and put it in the lock.

"Honestly, you're going to love what I've got to tell you! You know how you love science? The planets and how things work and . . . sound waves and, um . . . yeah . . . stuff. You know how you like all that and you find it all fascinating? Well, what I've got to tell you will *blow* your mind. Trust me!"

I fired a massive grin at him, but he looked unimpressed.

"What are you on about? Science is my worst subject. I hate it," he said. He opened his front door and stepped inside. "Just go away, will you? I don't even *know* you. My mum will be back any minute now, and she won't like you being here."

I stepped a bit closer.

"No, she won't. Your mum doesn't finish work until six and she doesn't get in until at least six thirty."

Charlie frowned at me. I carried on.

"I know it's going to sound crazy, but something happened and . . . actually, you'd better brace yourself for this. It might come as a shock."

Charlie raised his eyebrows.

"So, what happened is this: Somehow, and I'm really not sure how at the moment . . . somehow I have, um, managed to . . . erase myself from all existence."

Charlie stared at me and ran his tongue along the inside of his top lip as he sighed. He looked incredibly unimpressed.

"You're shocked! I can tell," I said. "I know. It's bonkers, isn't it? But it's true. And in my old life we were best friends. You and me! You were the dorky one, and I was the one getting into trouble all the time . . . and, well. Everything sort of went wrong. I accidentally broke your nose and ruined a big party at the school that was going to be on TV and . . . Well, none of that really matters anymore. I don't know *how*, but I wished I'd never been born, and just like that—I vanished. Well, not vanished, exactly, I'm still here, but now nobody knows who I am. I *really* have never been born. Can you believe it?!"

I laughed nervously, then swallowed as he stared back at me. He didn't say anything.

"I thought you might be able to help," I added, in a quiet voice.

He continued to stare at me and then he leaned against the doorframe and took a deep breath.

"I don't know what it is you're trying to achieve by making all this stuff up, but I'm not falling for it. Okay?"

My heart sank. This was my last hope, and it was going horribly wrong.

"Charlie, I'm telling the truth, I swear it," I said, fighting back the tears. "What do you think could have happened? Please? What can I do?! How can I get back?"

Charlie frowned.

"What can you do? Let me think . . ." he said. "It certainly is a dilemma."

I knew it! I just knew he'd have an idea in that big brain of his! I gave him a smile as he carried on.

"I know, how about you keep away from me and never come back? Does that sound like a plan?" he said. "Now get off my step and go home."

He went to shut the door, but I put my hand up and stopped him.

"But—But I don't *have* a home," I shouted.

He let the door go.

"Please, Charlie," I said. "This isn't a joke. I don't have anyone to ask. No parents, no friends, no grown-ups. *No one.* Please. I'm in trouble, BIG trouble, and I need your help. I need you to help me!"

I held my hands together like I was begging. His eyes flickered a little.

"We are really good friends, Charlie. The best! You've got to believe me."

He stared back. He didn't look angry; he looked almost embarrassed for me. Taking a deep breath, he leaned toward me, and I took a step closer.

"Leave me alone, you weirdo," he said, and the door slammed in my face.

I couldn't believe it.

I turned around and sank down onto the step. Now what? Reg couldn't understand, my sister was too terrifying to talk to, and if I tried to explain it to Mum or Dad, they would probably call the police and *then* where would I end up? It was no use. Charlie was my only hope. I just *had* to make him believe me.

I knelt down by the mail slot and carefully pushed it open with my fingertips. I could see the back of his head as he sat on the floor, untying his shoelaces.

"I'm going to go away in a minute and leave you alone, I promise. But before I do, I want you to listen to something. I know this is all hard for you to believe, but . . . just hear me out. Okay?"

Charlie sat motionless.

"When you were six years old, you went ice-skating with your cousins and you broke your wrist. You went to school with your arm in a cast, and everyone wanted to sign it. Davy Peterson wrote across it, in thick black pen: *CHARLIE IS AN IDIOT.* You managed to squeeze in a tiny *NOT* after the *IS*, but you were really upset about it."

I blinked as I watched him through the mail slot.

"If I didn't know you, how would I have known about that, eh?" I said.

He slowly turned, but his face was still frowning.

"But *anyone* could have told you," he said. "It wasn't exactly a secret. You might have asked my classmates about me, and they could have told you a hundred things. A *thousand* things."

He was right.

"Okay! Okay . . ." I shouted. "I'm trying, all right? I'm trying to get you to believe me, but I don't know how!"

Charlie shook his head.

"You're really not very clever at all, are you?" he said. The old Charlie would have never spoken to me like that, but at this precise moment I really didn't care. "Look. If you want to convince me, then you've got to tell me something that only you and I would know. If you'd been my best friend, like you say you were, I would have probably shared stuff with you and only you. Now, *that* would be proof."

This was why I needed Charlie's help. He was clever! I desperately thought of something else.

"Um . . . okay. I'm thinking . . . um . . . your favorite chip flavor is salt and vinegar?"

Charlie snorted. "Pathetic!" he said as he kicked off a shoe. "That could be a lucky guess."

"Um, how about the rarest bird that you've ever seen was a nightjar? You saw it at a nature reserve in Suffolk with your dad when it was his turn to have you for the weekend." He'd bored me for days about that one.

Charlie took his other shoe off.

"That's true," he said. "But again, you could have found that out from my parents. And anyway, bird-watching is boring. I only went because my dad dragged me there."

Well, that was rubbish, for a start. The Charlie I knew loved bird-watching. He stood up.

"Time's up," he said, folding his arms. "You need to go now or I'm ringing my mum."

"Hold on! I should get three tries. Everyone gets three tries of these kinds of things, don't they? Like in fairy tales!"

He glared at me through the mail slot. My fingers were beginning to hurt from keeping it open for so long.

"Come on then, Rumpelstiltskin," he spat at me. "Last try."

I thought hard. It had to be the best memory I had about him, ever. If I wanted to save Monster, I had to get this right. I needed to get home to save my dog.

"Right. Okay. I can do this," I said out loud. I cleared my throat. "On the back of the headboard in your bedroom, there's a drawing of a heart with *Charlie Loves Miss Jacobs* written inside it."

Charlie's jaw dropped.

"You had a crush on our fourth-grade teacher! You told me about it and showed me the heart when I had a sleepover at your house once."

I carried on.

"You said it was her long hair that you liked."

"But I've never told anyone about that, ever," said Charlie, his mouth dangling open.

I grinned through the mail slot. "But you did, Charlie! Me! And I never told anyone because, even though I wasn't the best friend in the world, I could keep a secret. Especially an embarrassing one."

Charlie walked across the hall, and I stood up. My knees throbbed from contact with the cold concrete step. The front door opened and Charlie stood there, still open-mouthed.

"Ohh, I've got another one," I said. "When we were about eight, you told me in class one day that you had a tummy egg. I remember thinking, *What's a tummy egg?* and then I realized you meant tummy *ache*. You'd been saying it wrong, like, *forever*. You were all embarrassed because you're so intelligent and stuff. You told me not to tell anyone, and I never did."

I grinned at him.

"Th-that's weird . . . yeah, I did used to say tummy egg." And then he frowned. "But I'm not intelligent, you got that bit wrong."

I shook my head.

"You are in my world. You know about all sorts of weird things, and you're interested in *everything*. You used to get picked on at school about it a bit, but I stuck up for you so the others left you alone."

He smiled. A tiny one, but it was still a smile. Something I'd said made sense.

"So . . . you said you've been erased? You didn't want to exist and you just . . . what? Disappeared from your own life?"

I nodded.

"And you're the smartest person I know. I figured if anyone can help me, then you can."

Charlie looked a little dazed as he chewed on his bottom lip, and then he suddenly opened the door wide.

"Look. I'm not saying I believe you or anything . . . but you'd better come in. And you've got to stop going on about this smart stuff, all right? I'm not clever."

"Okay, Charlie," I said, and I stepped into his house.

CHAPTER 31
CLOTHES

It was nice being back in Charlie's house. Everything looked exactly as I remembered.

"Have you got anything to eat? I'm starving," I said as I took off my shoes. Charlie's mum is the best cook in the whole world. She makes these amazing spicy samosas and these little flatbreads called chapatis. Charlie went off to the kitchen and came back with a sausage roll, a carton of juice, two cupcakes, and a banana.

"Oh," I said, staring at the plate. "Haven't you got any of your mum's food?"

"Don't push it," said Charlie.

I shrugged and stuffed the sausage roll in my mouth.

"Should we go and sit in your room, Charlie Geek?" I said, through chewed-up sausage.

He punched me hard on the top of my arm.

"What did you just call me?" he said, glaring at me. I rubbed where he'd hit. It had really hurt.

"Sorry. It was just a name we call you where I am from. It's not rude or anything. It's like a compliment, really. It's just because you're so clever."

He kept frowning at me.

"Don't call me that again. Okay? *Ever.*"

"Okay, Okay," I said, stepping away.

"Let's go to my room, and you can start from the beginning.

I'm not saying I believe you. I just want to see how far you'll go with this whole thing . . ." he said, frowning at me. I grinned at him through more sausage roll, but he didn't smile back.

———

Everything in Charlie's bedroom was different. The room I knew was extremely tidy, with science books lined neatly on his shelves and two plastic trays on his desk marked *Homework to Do* and *Homework Completed*.

This room was a mess. The shelves were cluttered with screwed-up pieces of paper, empty drink cans, and old cups. The desk was littered with schoolbooks, chip bags, and I counted seven empty plates. Even *my* room wasn't as bad as this. On the floor under the desk, I recognized a pile of illustrated encyclopedias that he'd gotten for his tenth birthday. I remember at the time I said that maybe he could take them back to the shop and swap them for something better, but he told me he'd actually *asked* for them. I gave him a hard time about that, but now, seeing them covered with a thick layer of dust, I just felt sad.

I sat on the edge of his bed and began to tell him about Reg and the old cabinet and the carved wooden egg full of strange things. I told him about the piece of sail from the spooky ship, the piece of Amundsen's glove, and Amelia Earhart's handkerchief.

"There was something else, too," I said, sucking the straw in the carton of orange juice. "A silver button."

Charlie stared back at me. He didn't look like he believed me, and he also didn't seem to be very interested. In fact, he looked like he was waiting for me to finish just so he could get rid of me.

"So, what do you think?" I said. "Should I take you to Reg's place and show you? You might get a few ideas once you've seen everything."

Charlie shrugged.

I finished the second cupcake, dropping crumbs down the front of my sweater. I brushed the crumbs off, which reminded me: "Can I borrow some clothes? I've only got these, and they're starting to stink a bit," I said.

Charlie tutted, then pulled open a drawer, throwing me a black sweatshirt; not exactly my look, but it'd have to do.

"Thanks," I said. I took my smelly sweater off and put the clean sweatshirt on over my T-shirt.

He leaned against the desk and scowled at me.

"I'm not saying I believe you, but if I did, what else is different?" he said. "You said I'm smart. What else?"

I sat on his bed.

"Everything. The school is run-down. My parents are divorced. My sister is Bex Beckett, and she's like some horrible bully here."

Charlie's eyes widened.

"Bex Beckett is your sister? Blimey."

I nodded.

"But she isn't like that in my world. In fact, she's the complete opposite. She's the most annoying Little-Miss-Perfect, never-done-anything-wrong-ever person you've ever met. She came to see the things in the cabinet yesterday. She knows a lot about history in my world, but here she pretends she doesn't. She's quite intellectual, actually."

Charlie rubbed at his eyebrow. "I find that hard to believe," he said, but I ignored him.

"My dad is still working in a job that made him so stressed he got ill. He looks like he is about to explode. And my mum . . . Well, my mum looks really happy and all that, but she's got a *boyfriend*."

We both grimaced.

"And have you tried telling them what's happened?"

I shook my head.

"No. Can you imagine? 'Hello, I'm the son you didn't know you had because I accidentally wiped myself out of existence. Oh, and can I come and live with you?' That's never going to happen. They'd call the police."

Charlie nodded.

"Also," I said, trying to keep my voice from cracking. "In my life I had a dog called Monster. A beagle. I saved him from being run over and now . . . now I can't find him anywhere."

Charlie nodded. "Yeah. That'll be because he's dead."

"Oh. Thanks for that," I said.

Charlie shrugged. "Sorry, Maxwell, but if you weren't there to save him, then he won't be alive, will he? Monster's gone. Everything you did in your world won't have been done here."

At least it sounded like he was starting to believe me.

"So, should we go? To see the cabinet?" I said. "I really think you're going to be able to help me with that big brain of yours, you know."

Charlie stood up.

"Okay. But I told you—lay off with all this 'big brain' stuff, okay? It's like you said, things are different here."

CHAPTER 32

BUTTON

On the way to Reg's, Charlie asked more questions.

"How about me? You said I'm clever, but is there anything else different about me in your world?"

I stuck my hands into my pockets.

"Um. Yeah. A little bit."

Charlie grinned and punched me on the arm again. It was really annoying when he did that.

"Go on, then. Tell me. What am I like?"

I shrugged.

"Oh, I dunno. You're just different. You've got a different hairstyle. You're more . . . you, I guess."

My best friend snorted.

"I'm not a dork or anything, am I?" He laughed. "Can you imagine it if I was a total nerd? Ha!"

Yes, you are, I thought in my head. *But I much prefer you that way.*

I kicked a stone and it rebounded off a garden wall and in front of Charlie's feet. Charlie kicked at the stone but totally missed. At least his sporting ability was the same.

"You never hung around with Marcus Grundy in my world, that's for sure. I don't understand why you're even friends with him! You hate him where I'm from."

Charlie shrugged.

"Marcus and I are buddies."

I tutted.

"Really? A friend that nearly strangles you in a headlock in front of the whole school?" I said.

Charlie forced a grin.

"Ah, he was only messing around!" he said, giving a faked laugh. "Marcus is like that, isn't he? He's just joking *all* the time. He's a joker."

I snorted.

"Well, I didn't see anyone laughing, did you? And in *my* world, you're really interested in science and you go to science club and read all these difficult books," I said. "Your latest thing is space, and you like to play me recordings of stuff on your headphones."

"Music?" he said.

I laughed.

"No. Nothing that normal. Apparently some scientists recorded the sound the sun makes and you played it to me the other day. It was *really* weird."

Charlie's eyes lit up.

"The sound the sun makes? Wow. I never knew they could do that . . . but I guess it's feasible . . ."

His forehead crinkled up like it did when he was thinking hard, but when he saw me looking, he shook his shoulders. It was as if he was trying to shake the real Charlie out of himself.

"Let's just hurry up and see what's in this cabinet, shall we?" he said, speeding up. "Let's see if we can get rid of you once and for all."

When we got to Reg's house, he was in the kitchen washing up. He looked a bit puzzled about who I was, but I quickly reminded him.

"This is my friend Charlie," I said, feeling Charlie bristle beside me. He clearly didn't like being called my friend. "I promised him he could have a look in the cabinet like Bex did. Is that okay? It's for a school project he's doing . . ."

I heard Charlie huff beside me, but Reg just smiled and nodded, then carried on washing up.

"What's wrong with him?" said Charlie as we went into the living room.

"He has problems with his memory," I said. "It's like his brain is a computer and it's accidentally been wiped clean and he can't access certain files anymore."

Charlie nodded as if he understood. I opened the cabinet, and his eyes lit up when he saw all the items.

"The really special things are in here," I said, taking the wooden egg and opening it up. I showed him the piece of sail. He knew about the *Mary Celeste*, and his eyes nearly popped out of his head when he held it. I then showed him the piece from Amundsen's glove and Amelia Earhart's handkerchief. By this point he was almost hyperventilating.

"This is unbelievable!" he said, inspecting each object really closely. "These things . . . they're . . . they are priceless. They should be in a museum!"

"It's good, isn't it?" I said, grinning. "I really think they must have something to do with me being erased, don't you?"

Charlie nodded quickly.

"Let me take a look at the egg?" he said. We sat on the floor and placed the open egg in front of us. Charlie studied each petal and read the writing on each side.

"*Louis Le Prince,*" said Charlie, reading the final section. "Who was he?"

I shrugged. "No idea," I said. Charlie took a phone out of his back pocket and began to search the name.

"Found him. *Louis Aimé Augustin Le Prince was a French artist and inventor . . .*"

He turned the phone around and showed me a black-and-white photograph of a man with a long mustache standing with his hand on a top hat. He looked very smart. Charlie scrolled down the page.

"He invented the motion-picture camera, apparently. Wow, why have I never heard of him? It says here that he recorded the first piece of film in 1888."

He kept scrolling and then stopped.

"Hold on, listen to this. *On the sixteenth of September 1890, Louis Le Prince boarded a train in France that was bound for Paris. When the train arrived, Le Prince had disappeared. No luggage or body was found on the train or along the railway track. He was never seen again.*"

I felt the color drain from my face.

"That's four disappearances. Four!" I said. "But it doesn't help me get back, does it?"

Charlie put his phone away.

"Were you near the egg when it happened?" he said.

"Yes! I was holding it! And I'm certain it made a noise. There's a music box inside."

Charlie looked at the small casing in the middle, then gave it a gentle shake. It rattled.

"Sounds like it's broken. Have you tried fixing it?"

I looked at him. "What do you think?" I said, folding my arms. "I'm useless. I broke the thing in the first place!"

Charlie squinted at the center of the egg.

"We've got to try and open it and see what's going on inside. There are some tiny gold screws."

He straightened up again.

"They're too small for a normal screwdriver," he said. "You could smash it open."

"Smash it? But then I might never get back!" I said.

Charlie sighed.

"I'm sorry, Maxwell. I don't know what to say. You need someone with special tools to help," he said.

I stared at him and gave him a grin.

"What?" he said.

I quickly put everything back in the egg and clambered up.

"I know exactly who can help!" I said. "Come on!"

CHAPTER 33
MAN

I ran to the main street, then slowed to a walk. I suddenly realized that the nice man in the shop might recognize me. He might have noticed that a phone case had gone missing and connected it to me. What if he called the police? I really needed his help, though. I had to take the risk.

"What's the rush?" said Charlie, catching up to me. "Where are we going?"

"The Fone Place. We need to get there before it closes," I said. I'd told Reg I was walking Charlie home. I hadn't told him I was taking the egg with me.

Charlie appeared to be in a daze. He wasn't listening to me.

"Is that really Amelia Earhart's handkerchief?" he said. "I can't believe it!"

He looked so happy.

"And that piece of Amundsen's glove! Wow. Well, that should definitely be shown to an expert. Maybe they could do some tests on it and date it to prove it's the right age. Don't you think?"

I had other things on my mind.

"To be honest with you, I don't really care. I just want to get home, and I'm not sure I can. My dog is dead, Charlie. He died because I wasn't there to save him. I *have* to get back."

We came to the Fone Place just as the lights turned off inside.

"Quick, he's locking up!" I said, pushing open the door. The man was walking across the shop with a big bunch of keys.

"Sorry, lads, I'm closed. I'll be open at eight a.m. tomorrow morning. Oh, it's you again," he said. I stared back at him, holding my breath as I waited for him to say something else. He had a slight smile on his face, and I relaxed a little when he didn't say any more.

"I'm sorry to bother you, but I need your help," I said. "I've got this musical egg and I really need to get it working."

The man pulled his jacket on and did up the zip.

"A musical egg, eh? I'm not sure if you've noticed, but this is a phone shop. You know? Those things you kids stare at all day?"

He chuckled to himself, and Charlie took a step forward.

"We just wondered if we could borrow one of your screwdrivers to open it up. It won't take a second," he said.

I held the wooden egg in front of me.

"Please?" I said.

The man sighed. "Come on, then, put it on the counter," he said. He went around the side and switched the lights back on, then got his glasses out of a case.

I placed the egg carefully on the counter. This was my only way of getting home, and I really didn't want it damaged any further.

"Wow, that's a beauty," said the man, studying the egg from all sides. "How do you open it?"

I pressed the little knob on the top, and the egg opened out. The bits were still inside, and I realized then that I probably should have left them back at Reg's, where they'd be safe. I picked them up and stuffed them in my pocket.

"I think this part at the bottom has a music box inside," I said.

"There are some tiny gold screws here and here," said Charlie, pointing at the box. "Have you got anything that will undo them?"

The man squinted at the screws, then looked at us over the rim of his glasses.

"No problem," he said. "Wait there." And he went out to the back of the shop.

Charlie looked at me when he was gone.

"I think we should ask him to try and fix it, too, don't you?" he said. "I don't know how these things work. I think he's your only hope."

I felt bad. The man who I'd stolen from was helping me more than anyone had helped me in the world. He came back with a little pouch and a small headlamp strapped to his forehead.

He grinned at us, then switched the light on before pointing his head down toward the egg.

"This requires a delicate operation," he said, removing a tiny screwdriver from the pouch. His tongue stuck out of the corner of his mouth as he twisted the egg around and began to undo the screws.

"We were . . . um . . . we were wondering," I said, "if you might be able to get it working as well."

The man breathed out slowly as he removed the tiny gold screw and put it to one side. He began to undo the other one.

"I see," he said. "You were in my shop the other day, weren't you?"

He put the screwdriver down and took off his glasses as he stared right at me. He knew. He knew I'd stolen the case. I dropped my eyes and nodded.

The man was quiet.

"I'd normally charge for this kind of thing, but I reckon you've kind of paid me already, don't you?" he said.

"I have?" I said. For a moment I wondered if it was some kind of trick and he was going to mention me stealing.

The man nodded and put his glasses back on as he picked up the dismantled egg and poked at it again with a tiny little screwdriver. "Yep. You told me about your friend listening to recordings of the sun. When I got home, I looked them up and listened to them myself. They're fascinating! Let's call that your payment to me, okay? You've helped me to discover something I never knew."

He gave me a kind smile and then looked back at his screwdriver. I looked at Charlie, and he grinned at me. Just then the man removed the other screw and lifted a piece of wood out of the egg. Underneath were the silver workings of the music box. He tipped the egg to one side, and a small piece fell out, along with a tiny roll of paper. Charlie reached over and picked it up, then slipped it into his trouser pocket. We both looked at each other. Was that piece of paper important?

"Fascinating! Such intricate work," said the man, peering at the music box. "It's just the rod that's come off. I should be able to attach it again."

Charlie and I watched as he reattached the tiny rod using a pair of tweezers. He stood back and closed the egg with a click.

"How does it play?" he asked. I held on to the egg and slowly twisted the little knob at the top. When I let go, music played for a few seconds from inside the egg. The man gave me a big grin as he put his tools away.

"Thank you! Thank you so much," I said.

"No problem at all," said the man. "Now, I really must close the shop. Off you go now."

⸻

As soon as Charlie and I got out of the shop, he took the small piece of paper out of his pocket.

"What is it? Is there anything on it?" I said, desperately trying to see over his shoulder. Charlie unrolled the tiny scroll. I could just make out some elaborate handwriting. He began to read:

"Four precious things,
Four notes to play
To erase yourself
From your very worst day."

We looked at each other, and then Charlie turned the piece of paper over.

"There's more!" he said. He began to read again.

"Four precious things,
Four notes to play
If you want to return
To that fateful day."

He looked up at me.

"That's it?" I said. "The four things and the four notes, that's all it took to erase me? And that is going to get me back?"

Charlie grinned at me.

"I guess so," he said. "I reckon you should try it now. To go back?"

"What, here? Now?" I said.

Charlie shrugged.

"Okay. Well, I guess there's no time like the present," I said. We got to a bench and sat down. I opened the egg on my lap and reached into my pocket to take out the things that I'd put away safely. I put them in the middle of the egg and closed it up until it clicked.

"Are you going to watch me, then?" I said, feeling awkward. Charlie shrugged again. I twisted the top of the egg, and the notes began to play. As the fourth note died, I whispered, "I wish I existed again."

I closed my eyes and then opened them. Charlie was still there, staring at me.

"Guess it didn't work," he said.

"But why? Everything is back as it was, *everything*."

"Let me see," said Charlie, taking the egg from me. He opened it up.

"So you've got the *Mary Celeste* sail, Amelia Earhart's handkerchief, Amundsen's glove . . . Where's the button?"

I stared at him.

"Louis Le Prince's silver button!" he said. I reached into my pocket to check if it was in there.

"It's gone!" I said.

CHAPTER 34

LOSER

My brain hurt while I thought back to the last time I'd actually seen the button. I didn't remember seeing it when I was showing the things in the cabinet to Charlie, but I did remember seeing it the time before that. There was only one culprit here, and it made me feel sick when I realized who it was.

Bex.

"I don't believe it," I said. "My own sister! Stealing from me right under my nose!" We walked back to Charlie's house. It *must* have been her.

"The button was the last thing I showed her, and then she acted all weird and suddenly rushed off," I said. "She must have been planning it all along. She wasn't interested in the things after all, she just wanted to steal something!"

Charlie was silent for a moment.

"You'll have to get the button back. There's no other way around it. If all those things are together, then maybe they have some kind of power that—"

He stopped. Someone was heading toward us, and Charlie was staring straight at them.

"Just keep your mouth shut," he whispered to me. It was Marcus Grundy with his little gang of numbskulls.

"What's up, Charlie?" said Marcus. He looked at me, and a sneer creased his top lip.

"Nothing much," said Charlie. "Just going home."

Marcus stared at me. "You're that loser from school, aren't you? The one who thought it was funny to shout lies about me across the playground."

I smirked at him. "They weren't lies, though, were they, Marcus? Would you like me to remind you what happened?"

He tried to stare me down for a bit but gave up.

"Right, well. We've got somewhere to be. Haven't we?" The boys around him did a group grunt and then he pointed a finger at Charlie's face.

"You might wanna have a think about who you hang around with, bro," he said, and they all slouched off.

Charlie put his head down and walked on.

"I don't know why you're friends with him," I said. "He's really not your kind of friend *at all*."

"Just shut up, okay?" said Charlie. "You don't know anything about who my kind of friend is, or my life, or *anything*."

I stumbled a bit as I tried to keep up with him.

"Oh yeah? Well, I *do* know you are a lot happier in my world. You're not trying to be someone you're not. You're not one of the cool kids, Charlie. And the sooner you realize that, the better!"

Charlie stopped and faced me.

"Look. I don't care who you are, or whether you get home to your make-believe world, or wherever it is you crawled from. But don't start telling me how to live my life. It's none of your business."

I couldn't believe it. I was losing him!

"What? I thought we were friends," I said.

Charlie shook his head.

"Don't be stupid. I don't ever want to see you again, all right? Got that into your thick head, have you? Has it sunk in?"

He tapped me on the head like he was checking I had a brain.

"But . . . what about my dog? You've got to help me!"

Charlie laughed.

"There is no dog! I can't believe I fell for your stupid lies. Just go away and leave me alone."

I let him walk on a bit, and then I caught up to him for one last try.

"Please, Charlie! You've got to help me get home," I pleaded. But my old friend turned his back on me and walked away.

CHAPTER 35

EMILY

I walked slowly back to Reg's. I'd gotten so close to having my friend back, and now I'd lost him all over again. And my sister was a liar and a thief who couldn't be trusted. I had to get that button back. I got to the bungalow, opened the kitchen door, and went in.

"Is that you, Maxwell?" called Reg from the front room. I'd only been gone a little while, so it was easy for him to remember me this time. I went into the living room, and Reg was sitting in his armchair beside the gas fire. His smile dropped when he saw me.

"Whatever is the matter?" he said.

I sank onto the sofa and stared at the orange glow of the fire.

"I've . . . I've lost everybody," I said. "I've lost my family. My best friend. My dog . . . I've got nobody here. No one at all."

Reg looked at me and slowly nodded. "Ah. I see . . . I see."

"I don't know what to do, Reg. I don't know how to get back to them. I miss them all *so* much," I said.

Reg's eyes looked all watery. "I'm so sorry, Maxwell," he said. "It's hard when you lose someone you love."

I looked at the kind old man who was sitting in the chair beside me.

"Have you got a family, Reg?" I said. I'd never wondered if he had anybody else in his life. All the time I'd been visiting the old man, I didn't know of anyone else who checked in on him. He opened his mouth, but then he closed it again. I kept silent, waiting for him to carry on.

"My wife was named Emily," he said. "We were so happy and we loved each other very much."

He swallowed and then blinked a few times as he stared ahead at nothing.

"We did everything together. We had such a happy life."

I kept quiet. I hadn't thought much about Reg's life outside his bungalow. I'd never seen him go anywhere.

"We took a trip to Italy once. That was a wonderful vacation," he said with a smile. "Emily's sister, Alice, and her husband, Jack, came, too. We were the best of friends, the four of us, and we traveled around for a whole month. It was *wonderful*. What a beautiful country. Have you ever been?"

I shook my head. Reg was smiling, but his eyes were sad. He went to take a sip of his tea but changed his mind and put the mug down.

"Did . . . did something happen to Emily?" I asked.

Reg cleared his throat and blinked toward the other side of the room for a while.

"Emily got sick. Very sick. It was right before her thirty-second birthday."

I gripped my hands in my lap.

"The doctor knew something was wrong right away," continued Reg. "She sent her straight to the hospital and they did lots of tests and . . . the news wasn't good."

I could see he was very close to crying. I wasn't sure what to do if a grown-up cried. When Mum cried, she usually went into the bathroom and I never really had to do anything.

"I'm sorry," I said. That was all I could think of to say.

Reg looked over at me. He suddenly looked very, very old. My stomach churned, and I swallowed away a sick feeling that I had in my throat. I didn't want to hear any more, but at the same time I wanted to know what had happened. A tear trickled down his cheek. He didn't wipe it away, and I watched it reach his chin and then drop down onto his shirt, making a little gray circle.

"The doctors tried everything. They gave her lots of different drugs, but some of the medicines were so strong that they began to make her ill as well." His voice cracked and he wiped at his cheek. I got up and knelt on the floor beside him, reaching over to pat his hand.

"I . . . I'm so sorry, Reg. I didn't know. I'm so sorry," I said.

Reg stared ahead.

"Alice and Jack were absolutely devastated, too. We all tried to be positive, but Emily was so poorly, Maxwell, so very poorly," he said. "I slept in a chair beside her hospital bed every night. One evening she smiled at me, then closed her eyes, and the next morning she just didn't wake up."

I felt a large lump in my throat as I tried not to cry. I stared at Reg as he wiped the tears from his eyes with his fingers.

"I haven't thought about all this for so long," he said. "I thought I'd forgotten." He began to cry properly then: quiet, deep sobs. I sat on the floor beside him and I held his hand and I didn't say a word.

I didn't get much sleep that night. I kept thinking about Emily not waking up while Reg was sitting in a chair beside her. That thought went over and over and over in my head, and every time I tried to forget about it, it came back and made my brain hurt. The next morning I was exhausted. I lay on Reg's sofa and looked at the mantelpiece where my portrait of him should have been on display. All that was there was an empty space. I was a nobody now. I didn't exist, and I'd never felt so alone.

CHAPTER 36
CAR

The only place I could think of where I might feel less lonely was school. I risked being spotted, but then it would be worth it to see everyone going about their lives. There was something strangely comforting about that, just seeing everyone else carrying on as normal.

I got to school early, and the first bell had just rung. I stood by the tree as everyone piled toward the doors, chatting and laughing.

"Hey, Callum! Can I borrow your shin guards?" a boy shouted across the crowd. Another boy took his backpack off his back, unzipped it, pulled out some muddy shin guards, and passed them to him.

Two girls were walking arm in arm, giggling about something and whispering in each other's ears. Behind them was a boy who was walking and reading a book at the same time. He held the book up high, and it was only when he went in through the door that he closed it.

I stood by the tree and watched all these real people with their real lives having their normal day. I would have given anything to have joined them. I would have given anything to be the old Maxwell Beckett again.

The school door closed behind the last person, and then there was silence. It was just as if someone had suddenly turned a giant volume dial down.

I stood there for a moment and watched a few students through the window of a classroom as they found their seats. I could see their lips moving as they chatted to each other. The teacher came in, and everyone turned to face the front.

I watched as everyone got their books out of their bags, and then it started to rain. I was quite sheltered under the tree, but after a few minutes it got heavier and I could feel the cold rain hitting my head. I looked around for somewhere better to shelter. The gate to the parking lot was open, so I quickly ran across the grass.

Mr. Howard's car was in the usual parking space. I tried the passenger door and it opened, so I got in.

My foot crunched onto a plastic cup. The floor was littered with them, along with empty cardboard sandwich boxes and candy wrappers. On the back seat there was a pile of clothes. It smelled bad, too. I didn't think Mr. Howard was in a good place right now, and I suspected he spent a lot more time at school in his car than he should.

I sank down low in the seat and folded my arms as I listened to the rain drumming on the car roof. It was nice to feel warm and dry when it was cold and wet outside, even if Mr. Howard's car wasn't exactly cozy. I yawned and closed my eyes for a bit. It was probably a good time to have a little nap to make up for the bad night's sleep I'd had. I'd hear the bell ring for break, and I could get out of the car and back to the tree before anyone was out. I'd see if I could spot Charlie and get his attention.

I folded my arms and tucked my chin in and settled down.

The next thing I knew, I could hear a banging noise. It was like someone was hammering on the inside of my brain. I slowly opened my eyes. My head was pressed against the window, and someone was hitting the glass.

"What are you doing in my car?!"

It was Mr. Howard.

"Get out!" he said. I didn't know what to do, so I just pressed the lock down. His mouth gaped at me, and then he stormed around to the other side. I reached across to lock that side as well, but he opened it before I had a chance and he got into the driver's seat.

"Well?!" he said, his eyes bulging.

I opened my mouth but it hadn't woken up yet—not that I knew what to say. I looked out the window. It had stopped raining, and everyone was outside. It must have been break time and I hadn't heard the bell ring.

"And why are you not in school uniform? Who is your home-room teacher? I think we need to have a word with them, don't you?"

I took a deep breath. I was too tired to lie anymore.

"I don't go to this school. I don't go to *any* school," I said.

Mr. Howard frowned, studying my face.

"You were here the other day, weren't you?" he said.

I nodded. He glanced down and seemed to notice the state that his car was in. He quickly grabbed a few bits of rubbish off the floor and threw them onto the back seat.

"Come to the office with me and we'll make a few phone calls, okay? It's not right to just go climbing into a stranger's car," he said. He reached for his door handle.

"But you're not a stranger!" I said. "You're Mr. Howard."

My teacher turned back, frowning.

"You're the nicest teacher in the school. *Everybody* likes you. Especially Ms. Huxley."

Mr. Howard's jaw dropped.

"I'm sorry?" he said.

"Ms. Huxley! The Spanish teacher? The one that went to Australia because you were too *chicken* to tell her how you felt? Remember her?"

Mr. Howard flushed pink.

"I—I don't know what you're talking about," he said.

I looked back at the playground and spotted Charlie standing with Marcus. Marcus was dancing around on his toes like boxers do when they're in a fight. Suddenly he started throwing pretend punches, and one hit Charlie on the shoulder. He fell backward into the fence.

"What is wrong with everybody?!" I said, turning back to Mr. Howard. "Why can't *any* of you make good decisions without *me* being involved? Why didn't you talk to Ms. Huxley before she went to Australia? You didn't call her, did you?!"

Mr. Howard stared at me.

"I really don't think you know what you're talking about," he said.

I shouted over the top of him.

"Ms. Huxley asked you to tell her how you felt about her just before she went to Australia. But you didn't. You let her go. But in *my* world, you *did* tell her because *I* said you should."

Mr. Howard looked back at me and blinked.

"I can't believe you didn't tell her, sir! And now look at you! It looks to me like you've just been moping around acting sorry for yourself, when really you should get straight on the phone and tell her *exactly* how you feel."

I sat back and folded my arms. I knew I'd have to make a run for it in a minute, but I needed to catch my breath.

"B-but . . . how? How do you know all this?" he started.

"I can't explain that bit," I said, fighting tears of anger. "I know you, Mr. Howard, trust me. And I'm having a really bad week. I didn't sleep much last night and . . . and . . . I just needed a little nap and time to think. I got in your car because I knew how nice you are and that you probably wouldn't mind."

Mr. Howard opened his mouth and closed it again.

"You should call Ms. Huxley and tell her you've made a big mistake and that you love her. Okay? Will you do that? Will you promise me?"

I watched Mr. Howard's chin slowly move up and down as he nodded. I did a big huff, and then I got out of the car and ran.

CHAPTER 37
ANGEL

When I ran past the playground, Charlie had his face pressed against the fence. I stopped and stared. Marcus Grundy was behind him, holding his arm around his back. Charlie stared at me with his cheek all squished against the wire. I was about to shout at Marcus to let him go when I remembered how certain Charlie had been that he and Marcus were friends.

Fine.

If he wanted a friendship like that, then that was up to him.

"Maxwell! Wait up!" shouted Charlie through his squashed mouth. I ignored him and kept running.

I ran to the main street and headed to the library. Mr. Howard would have spoken to Mrs. Lloyd by now. They were probably already making phone calls to the authorities about a strange boy who appeared to have nowhere to go. It would only be a matter of time before they asked the pupils if anyone knew me, and Charlie and Bex knew exactly where I was staying.

I walked into the library and headed to the back behind the big bookcases. My heart sank. Bex was there. She was wearing her school uniform and sitting at a desk staring at a book. I marched straight up to her and she looked up.

"Didn't feel like school today, then?" she said. I shook my head. "Me neither." She wasn't smiling. "I rang the absence line and pretended to be my mum. It's so easy. How did you do it?"

I just shrugged.

"Have a seat if you like," she said, nodding to a chair beside her.

I sat down in silence, staring at her. I would have to play this right to get the button. It was my last chance to get home.

"You go to Green Mills High, too, don't you?" she said.

I nodded.

"I hate it there. It's so boring."

"Ah, it's not so bad," I said quietly. "It depends who your friends are, I guess."

She glared at me, then looked back down at her book.

"Why did you take the button, Bex?" I said, watching her. She kept her eyes on the pages.

"I don't know what you're talking about," she said.

"A rubbish thief and a rubbish liar," I said. I knew that the first sign of lying was being unable to meet a person's eyes, and she was certainly doing that right now. She looked up at me. Her face really, really didn't care, but her eyes did. She was blinking a lot, for a start. And I knew she only did that when she was upset.

"Are you stealing for someone, Bex? The nail polish, the phone case, and now the button . . ."

She rolled her eyes.

"What's it to you?" she said, dropping her head to one side. All this showing off was driving me mad. I felt my anger coming back again. Just like it had when I was in Mr. Howard's car. I leaned in toward her.

"Okay, I'm going to tell you something now, Bex, and it's going to sound so crazy, so utterly incredible, that it's going to be hard to understand. Okay? It'll properly blow your mind. Are you listening?"

She slumped in her chair.

"Don't talk to me like that," she said.

I gritted my teeth together.

"Just shut up and listen to me, all right?" I said. My nose flared as I pointed my finger at her. She nodded slowly.

"Okay. Now, pay close attention," I said. "I know you, Bex Beckett. I can't explain how, but I do. I know you very well indeed. I know that you don't like mushrooms, but you will eat them if they're on a pizza. I know that you find swimming underwater easier than on the surface. And I know that you memorized all the kings and queens of England when you were just six years old."

Her jaw dropped and she began to say something, but I put my hand up.

"Hold on, I haven't finished," I said. "I know you once had a spider in the corner of your bedroom that you used to call Malcolm, and I know that your mum and dad used to hate each other so much that they'd put Post-its on their food so that the other one didn't eat it."

I took a breath.

"What?" she said.

"Bex, your parents hated each other *so* much that they couldn't even share a carton of milk."

I waited for a moment as she stared back at me.

"B-but . . . how did you . . . ?"

"Don't worry about that now. The thing is, the Bex I know is really, really clever. She does history projects when she doesn't actually have to, and she loves school and learning. She's had a tough time from a girl called Claudia, but rather than just becoming one of her 'gang,' she became her own person."

A tear escaped from the corner of Bex's eye and slowly trickled down her cheek.

"The Bex I know wouldn't steal makeup or phone cases or a silver button from an old man. The Bex I know would be comfortable in her own skin, even if it meant taking the odd dig from those around her who felt afraid of her. That's why Claudia is mean to you, Bex: because she's afraid of you. Not this mean version of yourself, the other one. The clever one who lives a real life and doesn't care what anyone else thinks."

I leaned back on the chair. I suddenly felt really, really tired.

"Who are you, Maxwell?" she said, her forehead creased as she studied my face. "You look kind of familiar, now that I think about it. Like you could be my . . . cousin or something."

I pushed my chair back and stood up.

"Just call me your guardian angel," I said. Bex blinked at me. Her mouth opened and closed again, and then I left.

CHAPTER 38
TEA

When I got back to Reg's, I sat on the sofa with the egg in my lap. It was pointless trying again without the button. Bex had probably sold it by now. There was no hope. I was trapped here. I stared at the gas fire as Reg appeared from the kitchen carrying a tray of tea and cookies. I decided to try Reg's memory one more time.

"Where did your grandfather get this egg from again, Reg?" I asked.

He placed the tray on the little coffee table.

"Vietnam. He traveled the world three times and was always getting himself into scrapes. The story goes that he was challenged to a card game in a café in the back streets of Ho Chi Minh City. Somehow he ended up winning, but his opponents accused him of cheating and wouldn't pay up. He started getting into an argument with them but decided to make a run for it, grabbing that egg from a shelf as he went. He said that it was his payment."

"Isn't that stealing?" I said.

"Yes, I guess it is," said Reg. "He always said that egg ruined his life, so maybe he got his comeuppance anyway."

I held on to the egg and stared at him.

"What do you mean it ruined his life?" I said.

Reg thought about it for a bit.

"Oh, I don't know. He lost friends, I think. I don't really remember the details."

My throat tightened as I leaned forward on the sofa.

"What do you mean, he lost friends? Where did they go?" I said, almost whispering to him.

"Did I say lost? I don't know. I guess he fell out with them," he said cheerfully. "Like I said, he was a bit of a character . . ."

"But . . . did they disappear? The lost friends?" I said, my heart pounding. "Where did they go? Did they come back? Why haven't you told me about this before?!" I was shouting now.

Reg stared back at me. "I . . . I don't know, Maxwell. I guess I didn't think it was important."

My stomach was churning. I didn't say anything as I watched the old man sipping his mug of tea. He didn't seem to understand what I was asking.

"I've lost everyone, Reg," I said, feeling the tears coming. "*Everyone.* And Monster is dead, and it's all down to that stupid, *stupid* thing."

He looked over at me.

"I'm sorry you feel so upset, Maxwell. I know exactly how it feels," said Reg. "You see, when I lost my wife I—"

"I know," I said sharply. "You've told me that story already. It's very sad, and I'm very sorry you went through that. I don't know if you've noticed, but I've got *a lot* going on myself at the moment."

I didn't want to hear about Emily again. It was too upsetting. And besides, my mind was still trying to process what he had just told me about his grandfather's lost friends. Did that mean something? Had they disappeared as well?

"She died, you see. My wife, Emily . . ." said Reg, again.

"Reg, *I know*," I said. "You've already told me." I looked at the carved egg in my lap. If I could just figure out how to make it work without the button, then I could go home. But what if it wouldn't? What if I was trapped here, forever?

"I couldn't bear my life without her, you see," said Reg, his voice trembling.

I sighed and put my head in my hands as Reg carried on.

"After a while of being on my own, I made a big decision. A very big decision indeed."

I stared at the egg in my lap as I listened.

"I decided," said Reg, "I decided that I didn't want to stay in a life where Emily wasn't around anymore. I wanted to . . . escape . . ."

I peered at him through my fingers.

"I wanted a new life," he said. "I was looking to go to a place where there were no memories of Emily. To a place where nobody knew who I was."

I slowly took my hands away from my face and stared at Reg.

"That's when I did it, Maxwell," he said, staring straight at me, the whites of his eyes all shiny.

"Did what, Reg?" I said, almost as a whisper. He breathed in and out: once, twice, three times, before he finally answered me.

"That's when I erased myself," he said.

CHAPTER 39

GRANDFATHER

Reg blinked at me as I stared back at him. My mind raced as I tried to process what he'd just told me.

Reg?

Reg had been *erased*?

The old man sitting in his armchair had been erased? Just like me?

He had no friends, no family, and no visitors. There were no photographs of his family on the mantelpiece, nothing. Surely he would at least have had a picture of his wife somewhere. But there was nothing. There was *nothing* here that showed the man's past. His history. His life.

I stood and paced around the carpet.

"I . . . I don't understand . . ." I said. "You? *You* wished you'd never been born?"

Reg slowly nodded his head and put his hand to his chest, and his face flushed.

"I feel a bit strange," he said. "I haven't told anyone, you see. I haven't spoken of this ever since it happened."

I couldn't stop staring at him. Was that why his memory was so bad? Because he'd erased himself?

"What happened, Reg?" I said calmly. He looked up at the ceiling as he thought about it.

"My grandfather lived in this bungalow for many years after his travels. Have I ever told you that?"

I shook my head, speechless.

"All the things here belong to him. This armchair, that sofa, the cabinet. It's hard to start another life when nobody knows who you are. You don't have any identification, nowhere to live, no friends to ask for help, no family. Nothing."

I knew that feeling all too well. Reg carried on.

"But then there's also no painful reminders of happier times. The kind of thing that can catch you unexpectedly, like her favorite cup on the shelf or a silver hairclip in the drawer. Seeing something that simple can completely take your breath away with grief."

Reg swallowed and rubbed his eyebrow.

"When you're erased, there are no photographs, no diaries, no reminders of your previous life. There's nobody knocking on the door or calling you three times a day to check if you're okay. I wanted this life where nobody knew who I was. I wanted some peace."

I stared at Reg as I listened to him talking. He really did think that erasing himself was the answer. It was so sad. But I didn't want to end up like him. I wanted to go home.

"And it was this egg that made you disappear, wasn't it?" I said, holding it up. "The things inside make it happen."

He frowned as he rubbed his forehead.

"I—I don't know."

"But you must know. Something is missing inside, and you've

got to help me find something else to replace it," I shouted. "You've got to help me, Reg, please!"

Reg looked back at me, puzzled. I dug my nails into the palms of my hands.

"I . . . well, I'm not sure . . ."

I got off the sofa and dropped down onto my knees at his side.

"I don't want to be erased anymore, Reg. Don't you understand? I want to go home!"

I put my head down and sobbed. I cried and I cried. I felt his hand gently pat me on the head.

"I'm sorry, Maxwell. It all happened such a long time ago," said Reg.

I dabbed at my eyes with the cuff of my sleeve.

"I just wanted . . . I just wanted the chance to go back and see everyone and tell them . . . and tell them how much I love them, you know?"

I looked up at him.

"Haven't you ever wanted that, Reg? To see your family and friends again?"

Reg shook his head.

"I don't know. I can't really remember my old life, Maxwell. It's all . . . foggy. I don't exist there."

I thought of the life he had now, surrounded by things that didn't really belong to him, with no friends and no family.

"But you don't really exist in this world, either, do you?" I said. "This world is even emptier than your old one."

He blinked back at me. This would be how I would become

one day, too. An erased man with no past and nothing in his present.

"I know it was painful back there, but you had people around you who loved you," I said. "What about Alice and Jack? They are still there. Why don't you—"

I stopped as the back door flew open.

"Maxwell? Are you there?"

Charlie burst into the living room and ran toward me. I stood up, and he grabbed me by the shoulders. He was grinning.

"Maxwell Beckett, I'm going to get you home!" he said.

CHAPTER 40
BOX

As Charlie walked into the room, I realized there was someone behind him. It was Bex. She looked at me all sheepishly.

"Maxwell?" she said.

Charlie looked at me.

"I hope it's okay, but . . . I kind of told her who you are. To get the button back."

I looked at her as she took a deep breath.

"Is it true?" she said. I nodded. Her mouth opened and it stayed like that, in a little dark circle.

"I live with you, Mum, Dad, and a dog called Monster," I said. "A lovely, chubby, funny beagle who means everything to me. You like history, and you like wearing black and gray, and you definitely don't wear orange makeup or shoplift or skip school. That's how I know all that stuff. Because you're my sister, Bex."

She blinked a few times and then swallowed.

Charlie paced around the carpet, waving his hands up and down as he talked. He looked *exactly* like the Charlie back in my real life. Even his hair had lost a bit of its spikiness.

"And she's got the button! Show him, Bex!" My sister fumbled in her blazer pocket and held it out in her palm. I took it from her and gripped it tightly in my hand.

She looked embarrassed for a moment and then perked up when she saw the cabinet.

"You do realize that if those things in that egg are real, then it's possibly one of the most important finds in decades," she said. "It must be worth hundreds of thousands."

"I suppose so," I said. "But I don't care about that. I just want to get home."

She nodded at me.

"I'm sorry I took it. It was stupid. I just did it in the spur of the moment. It's only when Charlie explained what was going on that I realized how important it is," she said. "Even if it does all sound a bit . . . far-fetched."

I shrugged.

"That's okay. I've done far worse things to you in my life," I said. She suddenly held her hand out toward me.

"Well, if you get back, I think you should promise to be nicer to your big sister. Do we have a deal?"

I hesitated, then shook her hand.

"Deal," I said. I turned to Charlie. "Thanks, Charlie. For telling Bex," I said. "I'm glad you came back."

"You were right about Marcus," he said. "He is a complete idiot. I'm going to steer clear of him from now on."

I grinned at him.

"Look, can you guys wait in the kitchen for a moment? I just need to have a chat with Reg." They both looked at me and then at the old man and nodded. They went out to the kitchen and closed the door behind them.

Reg was sitting in his armchair with his arms folded across his tummy. I went over and sat beside him.

"Have you ever wanted to go back, Reg? Back to your real life?" I asked him.

Reg looked at me with sadness in his eyes. And then he shook his head.

"Well, I can't stay here," I said. "I've got to get home to my family. To my *real* family. I miss them, Reg. I thought I wasn't good enough. I thought things would have been better for everyone if I'd just never been born. But . . . I was wrong. I *am* important, Reg. They do need me. And I . . . I want to go home."

What was going to happen to me? I couldn't live here forever. Reg looked at me and smiled.

"I think you'll find a way home, Maxwell. And do you know why?" he said.

I shook my head.

"Because you feel it in here," he said, patting his chest.

His eyes filled with tears. It must have been so hard to say that—that the world was better off without him in it. But then I'd felt that myself, hadn't I? And now it couldn't be further from the truth. I picked the egg up from the sofa and took it over to the cabinet. I could hear Bex and Charlie talking in the kitchen, but I didn't want them to be here when I tried. I wanted to do this on my own.

I looked at the egg in my hands. This was it. This was my moment to get home. I *was* important—I could see that now. It was because of me that my dad had left the job he hated, that Bex was her real, true self who loved history, and that Mr. Howard and Ms. Huxley were in love and together. If I got home, I'd have a chance to tell the school how sorry I was for all the trouble I'd caused and for ruining the biggest night of the year. And I'd make it up to Charlie, my best friend in the whole wide world. I'd tell him how sorry I was that I wasn't always the nicest friend to him and that I would be better from now on. But better than all those things was the thought of my dog. If I got back, then Monster would be alive again.

I took a deep breath and pressed the top of the egg, and it slowly opened. I put the button inside with the other pieces and carefully closed it. I then twisted the tiny knob on the top, and the music box inside played its four notes.

"I want to exist again," I said just as the notes stopped. I looked at my reflection in the glass cabinet door. I didn't feel a thing. I didn't feel any different in the slightest. I sighed as I opened the cabinet and put the egg back on the shelf beside the black hat.

Reg was asleep in his armchair when I turned around. He must have nodded off. I stood and watched as his chest gently rose and fell. The bungalow was almost silent. All I could hear was Reg's gentle snoring.

I went to tell Charlie and Bex that it hadn't worked, but when I got to the kitchen, they weren't there.

"Charlie? Bex?" I said.

I hadn't heard them leave. Where were they? I opened the door and looked down the path, but there was no sign of them.

My heart began to pound.

I ran into the living room, looking around, and spotted it straightaway. It was back on the mantelpiece where it always should have been.

"I don't believe it!" I shouted. Reg jumped awake.

"What's that . . . what's going on . . . ?" he said, pushing himself up out of his chair. I ran over to him and gave him a hug.

"What's going on?" he said, laughing nervously. I held on to his hands and did a little jig.

"It's me, Reg! It's Maxwell!" I said, trying not to laugh.

I went over to the mantelpiece and picked up the framed drawing that I'd done of Reg. The picture of something in my town that I was most proud of. The one that had won first prize. I gripped it between my hands, grinning as my heart raced in my chest.

"I'm back!" I said.

CHAPTER 41
WAVING

I left Reg standing in the middle of his living room, staring at the portrait.

I ran down his path and turned right, past Mrs. Banks's front garden. Mrs. Banks was on her bright green lawn, trying to reattach the flamingo's head onto its body using parcel tape.

I stared as I gripped her fence.

"IT'S THE HEADLESS FLAMINGO!" I shouted. "YES!"

I did a little air punch as Mrs. Banks glared at me. I waved at her.

"Hello, Mrs. Banks! It's me, Maxwell!" Her jaw hung open.

"I'm going to mend your flamingo, Mrs. Banks!" I shouted. "And if I can't mend it, then I'm going to buy you another one with my pocket money. I'll buy you the best flamingo you've ever seen! How about that?"

Mrs. Banks appeared to be frozen to the spot as I gave her another big grin before I ran on. There was someone I needed to see first before I went home—Charlie. If it hadn't been for him, I'd have never gotten back. I sprinted to his house, and by the time I got to the front step I was out of breath. As I pressed the doorbell, I looked at the corner of the garden—Dirt-Track Mountain was back. I smiled to myself, but Charlie's mum certainly wasn't smiling when she opened the door and saw me. She immediately went to shut it again, but I put my hand up to stop her.

"I'm sorry I hurt Charlie's nose, Mrs. Kapoor. It really was an accident, but I don't blame you for not believing me. I haven't been the best friend to Charlie, have I?"

Mrs. Kapoor was about to say something when Charlie appeared behind her wearing a navy suit with a huge bandage across his nose. Of course! The school's Hundredth Anniversary Celebration! Days had passed for me in the other world, but somehow I must have come back at exactly the same point I'd left. His hair was in its usual wild state and it looked brilliant.

"Charlie!! You're back! Hang on, what am I saying? I mean *I'm* back!" I said, laughing. Charlie and his mum just stared at me.

"And your nose! You've got the bandage on. Isn't that brilliant?" I laughed again, but stopped when nobody joined in. Mrs. Kapoor put her arm around Charlie's shoulder.

"Charlie isn't going to be hanging around with you, Maxwell. You're a bad influence and not a true friend. Isn't that right, Charlie?" she said.

I looked at Charlie, who dropped his eyes and nodded.

"Okay, Mrs. Kapoor. I understand. But can I just talk to him on my own? Just for a minute?"

She scowled at me.

"One minute," she said sternly, and she went inside. As soon as she'd gone, Charlie started talking.

"You're in big trouble, Maxwell," he said. "I wouldn't be surprised if they expel you for what you did at the ball."

"Expel me?" I said. Of course. I'd turned the electricity off and ruined it for everyone. I hadn't even thought about the consequences of that. Charlie carried on:

"And Mum was right. I don't want to hang around with you anymore. You've done nothing but make me feel bad about myself. Do you realize that? No. Of course you don't. Because you only ever think about yourself, Maxwell Beckett. Don't you?"

I went to disagree, but he hadn't finished.

"And I know you're only friends with me because there isn't anyone else stupid enough to hang around with you. But to be honest with you, I think I'd rather be on my own now."

He folded his arms, waiting for me to say something.

"Oh. I see . . ." I said.

"Do you see, though, Maxwell? Do you *really*? Because all these years you haven't *seen* once, have you? You only ever *see* yourself."

I nodded at him slowly.

"Yes. Yes, you're right," I said. "I've been a terrible friend."

Charlie shifted from foot to foot as he stared at the floor. I continued:

"I've been horrible. I've laughed at you behind your back, and I've let you down. I don't expect you to want to be friends with me ever again, but I just wanted to say . . . you're my best friend, Charlie. You are funny and brilliant and clever and . . . and I guess I've probably been a bit jealous of you. How you never get in trouble and you know so much . . . *stuff*. And you always seem to be happy just being *you*, you know? You don't care what anyone thinks of you. Not in this world, anyway . . ."

Charlie looked up at me, a puzzled look on his face, but he quickly looked back down.

"I won't hang around with you anymore if that's what you

want. Okay? But if you do ever want to be friends again, then let me know."

I waited for him to say something, but he didn't even look at me. I dropped my head and turned away, and as I walked down the pathway I heard the front door close behind me.

CHAPTER 42
HOME

I left Charlie's house feeling sick. I wasn't surprised he was angry with me, but I wasn't prepared for him not wanting to ever be friends with me. His mind was clearly made up, and there was no way he was going to change it.

I turned toward my street and put my hands in my pockets. My fingers felt something cold, and when I took it out I saw it was a key. The key to the boiler room at school that I'd locked after I'd turned the electricity off. I hadn't really given much thought to the fact that I was going to be in a whole heap of trouble after what I'd done at the ball. What would happen if I got expelled? I'd have to go to a new school, and who would want to be friends with someone like me?

My house was up ahead, and when I got to our path, I stopped. The gate was missing. The one I'd swung on all those years ago and broken. I gave the gatepost a little pat as I walked past.

Mum opened the door just as I arrived. She looked livid.

"Maxwell! What on *earth* have you done? Do you realize how dangerous that was? Turning the electricity off at school? With all those hundreds of people there?"

Dad appeared behind her, and Bex came downstairs in her jeans and gray HISTORY AIN'T DEAD T-shirt. She was back to normal again.

I stood there for a moment and looked at my family, and then I threw my arms around my mum.

"I love you, Mum, I love you all. I'm so sorry for everything. I'm so sorry for everything that I've done wrong."

Mum slowly wrapped her arms around me and rubbed my back.

"What's the matter, Maxwell? What's happened?"

I pulled away from her and then threw myself into my dad's arms.

"Dad, it's so good to see you. I'm sorry you're both so miserable."

I could see my sister's face over my dad's shoulder. She looked worried. I gave her a smile, and she smiled back. Even though things were probably about to get a whole lot more complicated, it was so nice to be back with my family.

There was still someone left to see. The kitchen door behind Bex gave a shudder and burst open as my fat, funny, happy beagle thundered toward me.

"Monster!" I said, letting go of Dad and dropping to my knees. My dog threw himself into my open arms, his tongue dangling out of the side of his mouth like it always does.

"I've missed you, Monster! I missed you so much," I said, burying my face in his neck. He smelled absolutely awful and so, so good.

"Maxwell? What's going on? Are you okay?" said Mum.

I kissed the top of Monster's head and turned around and looked at my family. They all stared back at me, confused looks on their faces.

"I'm fine, Mum. I'm absolutely fine," I said.

I suggested that I should go straight to school and own up to turning off the electricity and ruining the whole evening. Not that I needed to own up—it was pretty obvious who had done it. Mum and Dad were both a bit shocked to hear what I wanted to do, but they agreed.

Dad drove us there and parked where the TV truck had been. Everyone had packed up and gone home now. There were a few people hanging around in the playground, including Mrs. Lloyd. I told my parents that I wanted to talk to her alone, so they waited for me in the car. As I walked across the playground, Mrs. Lloyd spotted me straightaway and folded her arms.

"Well, well, well, Maxwell Beckett. Don't *you* have a lot of explaining to do." She looked like she could breathe fire, but something about my face made hers soften a little.

"Mrs. Lloyd, I'm sorry I ruined everything with the TV company and the ball. I . . . I was just so upset I couldn't come. I'm so sorry."

I took the key to the boiler room out of my back pocket. Mrs. Lloyd came a step closer and took it from me.

"This can't carry on, Maxwell. Your behavior was reckless and dangerous and it ruined a perfectly nice evening for a lot of people. I'm going to have a serious think over the weekend about how we can resolve your continuing bad behavior."

I nodded.

"Come and see me first thing on Monday morning. I'll need your parents to be there, too. Both of them," she said.

"I know, miss. I understand. I'll see you on Monday."

I turned and walked back to my family.

CHAPTER 43
OFFICE

On Monday, I went straight to Mrs. Lloyd's office with Mum and Dad. Mr. Howard was there as well, and everyone's faces looked tense and like they were about to shout at me. I wasn't feeling very hopeful. Mrs. Lloyd started by reading from my school file, which they must keep in the office. It included a record of all the trouble I'd been in over the past year. It went on and on and on. I even saw Mr. Howard flinch a couple of times. Mum let out a huff now and then, and Dad glared at the carpet.

"Do you have anything to say, Maxwell?" she said, closing the file. "Do you really hate school that much that you'd spoil every day that you are here?"

I'd been thinking about what I was going to say all weekend. I'd told Charlie how I felt, and I'd told Mum, Dad, and Bex how much they meant to me. And now it was the school's turn. I cleared my throat.

"I don't hate school," I said. Mrs. Lloyd rolled her eyes, but Mr. Howard leaned forward with his elbows on his knees, his fingers pressed to his mouth.

"In fact, I like school. School is my 'normal.' It's my place to get away from . . . from the shouting at home."

I felt Mum flinch. There was no way I could look at her or Dad. I cleared my throat again. "I know I haven't been the best pupil, or the best friend, or the best son. But I do care. I care about my friends and my family, and even my school. I just . . . I just sometimes do stuff to ruin it. You know?"

Mr. Howard was the only one nodding. I carried on.

"School is a place where things are okay. Where there aren't two people shouting across my head or trying to ruin each other's lives or sticking stupid Post-its onto their food."

Mrs. Lloyd glanced at Mum and Dad, but they didn't say anything.

"And sometimes when I come to school I feel like I'm a bottle of fizzy drink. All evening or all weekend I've been trying to keep the lid on the bottle, but that bottle . . . that bottle feels like it has been inside a washing machine and it's fit to burst. Do you know what I mean?"

I looked at my teachers. I don't think they really did know how it was to feel like a bottle of fizzy drink, but they both nodded. I took a deep breath.

"And then, when I get to school, I sit back and *WHOOOSSHHH!* It's like . . . it's like the lid just blows off . . . just like that. And all my thoughts and worries and upsets . . . well, they all come shooting out, and I can't . . . I can't get the lid back on again."

I noticed that I was twisting my hands together and it kind of hurt, so I stuffed them underneath my knees. Mrs. Lloyd's face didn't look quite as angry, and Mr. Howard was pressing his lips together. Dad cleared his throat but didn't speak.

"I'm sorry for everything I've done, Mrs. Lloyd." My voice began to wobble then, so I stopped there.

My principal sat back in her chair.

"I think . . ." she said. Her eyes looked up at the ceiling for a moment. She seemed to be struggling to find the right words. "I think that you are a clever, intuitive, and understanding young boy, Maxwell. And I think . . . I think Mr. Howard and I need to have a good chat with your parents about how we can try and help with all this frustration you're feeling. How does that sound?"

I opened my mouth and closed it again. Mr. Howard leaned forward.

"I think we can all work together and learn something from each other here. Us as teachers, your parents, and you. Isn't that right, Mr. and Mrs. Beckett?"

I looked at Mum and Dad. They looked awkward, but they nodded.

"Does that mean I can stay at this school?"

Mrs. Lloyd started fiddling with some papers on her desk.

"You'll still be punished for what happened at the ball—we can't let that go. But we won't be taking things further than that. Now, get yourself off to your first lesson and . . . be good. Okay, Maxwell?"

I nodded back, trying not to grin too hard as it kind of hurt my cheeks.

———

My punishment for turning the electricity off at the ball was to help Mr. Farrow, the caretaker, with his duties during break times for a few weeks. I walked around the playground picking up litter while wearing an orange jacket. The other kids thought it was hilarious and shouted stuff at me, but whenever I felt like shouting back, I thought about being erased and kept quiet. I also had one of those little grabbers, and after a while I quite enjoyed spotting a candy wrapper, picking it up with the claw, and putting it in my trash bag. I found I was concentrating on what I was doing so much that the bell would ring before I knew it.

I was also on "report," which meant I had to get a card signed after each class to say if I'd behaved myself during the lesson or not, and if I got any negative points, then I would be back in Mrs. Lloyd's office. I knew I wouldn't get into trouble again. I was hoping to try and talk to Charlie, but he was at a hospital appointment getting his nose checked again, so that made me feel a whole lot worse.

On my way home from school, I prepared myself for Mum and Dad to launch into another argument after the meeting with Mrs. Lloyd. I knew they'd be blaming each other for everything, especially the bit about me feeling like a fizzy bottle. But when I got in everything was quiet. Dad was in the kitchen making dinner, and Mum was sitting at the table on her laptop. They weren't talking, but it didn't feel tense like they'd had a big fight or anything. It just felt like they'd run out of things to argue about.

Monster came over to greet me like he always did, wagging his tail around and around, and I gave him a longer cuddle than usual.

"Someone dropped this off earlier," said Dad, handing me an envelope.

I stared at the envelope that had *MAXWELL* written on the front. I recognized the handwriting immediately. I was going to go to my room to open it when Dad suddenly put his arms around me and squeezed me.

"We love you, Maxwell. We both love you very much indeed."

I squeezed him back, and then I went over to Mum and gave her a big hug, too. She held my face in between her hands.

"We're very proud of you, Maxwell. We might not show it sometimes, but we really are," she said. And she gave me a wet kiss on my cheek that I quickly wiped off.

I kicked my shoes off and ran upstairs with the letter.

I dived onto my bed, ripped the envelope open, and began to read.

Dear Maxwell,

You are right. You are a terrible friend.

   You've lied to me, you've laughed at me behind my back, and you've made me feel like you're only friends with me because no one else wants you. And let's face it—who would be stupid enough to be friends with you?

I stopped reading for a moment. I didn't think I could face being told how awful I was anymore. I took a glimpse at the next line, then carried on.

   But then there are things about you that I kind of like. When you're not messing around, you can really make me laugh. I like it when I sometimes tell you something I've learned, which I think you might be interested in, and you look happy because you seem pleased that I've decided to tell you rather than someone else. And also, you make me feel like I know more stuff than anyone else in the world, and that makes me feel kind of good.

I've been to the hospital today, to get my nose checked (it's fine by the way), and while I was waiting to be seen I decided that I'm going to give you another chance. Another chance at being my friend.

So, I'm writing to ask you—can you try and not mess it up this time?

And can you stop calling me Charlie Geek? It really gets on my nerves.

From your long-suffering friend,
Charlie <u>Kapoor</u>

I smiled to myself as I folded the letter and put it into the envelope again. Charlie was back.

CHAPTER 44
APARTMENT

About six weeks after I returned to my real life, everything changed.

Dad moved out.

My parents sat with me and Bex one evening and talked about how they both loved us very much indeed, but they didn't love each other as much as they used to. They said that they were tired of arguing with each other, and that it wasn't fair to us, and that they were both sorry that it had been going on for so long. They'd come to an agreement about money, and Dad could afford to move into a little apartment. He wasn't moving too far, and we'd still see him a lot. They said there might come a time when we'd have to sell the house, but if that ever happened, they promised that we wouldn't go far and that we could stay at the same school. Bex cried when they told us. Mum gave her a big hug, but she didn't say anything. I felt sad but okay. I'd seen how happy Mum had been when I'd been erased and, even though I'd much rather she loved Dad again, I wanted to see her smile. And in this world, Dad had a job that he loved, so I hoped that he would be all right, too.

We saw Dad for one evening during the week and every other weekend. At first he didn't seem to take it very well. His apartment was tiny and smelled a bit, and he didn't make any effort to keep it tidy. Also, when he dropped us home, he'd hug us for a really long time. It was like he didn't want to let us go. But after a few weeks I noticed that he'd bought some lamps for the apartment and put some pictures on the wall. He also joined a squash league at the sports club, and apparently he was quite good at it. He said he'd take me and Bex one day and show us how to play. When he'd come to pick us up, he used to wait outside in the car, but last weekend, while I was still packing my bag, Mum invited him in and I could hear them talking in the kitchen. I came down and they were drinking coffee, and Mum was laughing about something Dad had said. I hadn't seen them like that since . . . well, I couldn't even remember. The fridge was now a sticky-label-free zone, which suited me fine.

Charlie and I were friends again, and I never called him Charlie Geek anymore; I kept my word about that. And I tried to be a really good friend. Sometimes he'd go off on a ramble in class about something he knew loads about, and everyone would groan and moan about him being boring. Normally I'd have elbowed him in the ribs and told him to stop being an idiot, but now I'd glare at everyone else and they'd eventually shut up.

It took him a while to trust that I was being a true friend, and I think he started to believe it when we had field hockey in PE one day. Mrs. Allen began the lesson by teaching us how to dribble with the ball, but Charlie couldn't control it, and he kept tripping over his stick. We had to get into teams for a match and it was up to me and Adel to pick our players. Charlie was, by far, the worst in the class, but I picked him first, which made everyone gasp, including him. He might have been a rubbish player, but there isn't anybody else I'd rather have on my side.

One day I'll tell him about what happened, maybe when we're

old men, sitting on a bench drinking tea from a thermos. Maybe then I'll tell him how he helped to bring me home.

I still saw Reg every few days. He struggled with his memory more and more, and it took me a lot longer to explain who I was. On some days he just didn't understand who I was at all, so I left him alone then. I didn't want to upset him. When he was having a good day, I carefully asked him about the old life that he'd left behind, although I never mentioned him being erased. One day in the winter, we were sitting around his gas fire in the living room and he began to talk.

"I had a very peculiar dream last night, Maxwell," he said. "It was about a young man who had lost someone he really, deeply loved."

I held tightly on to my mug of hot chocolate as he spoke in his soft voice.

"Now, this man," continued Reg, "well, he found it very hard to live without this other person in his life. He thought everything was pretty pointless, and then one day he just disappeared . . ."

Reg *poofe*d his hand in the air. I stayed silent.

"But he hadn't disappeared completely. He was in the same surroundings, but nobody knew who he was. He got a chance to see this strange world, a world in which he had never been born, and he saw the differences he had made to his friends' and his family's lives. And then he realized something."

Reg's voice shook a little.

"What, Reg?" I whispered. "What did he realize?"

The old man turned toward me, his brow creased with lines.

"He realized he wanted to go home," he said. He took a deep sigh and put his hot chocolate down on the table.

"Do you want to go home, Reg?" I asked, putting my hand on his arm.

He looked at me, and his bottom lip trembled.

"I—I don't know," he said. "I'm frightened."

If Reg went back to his old life, then he'd be returning to the worst moment ever. Emily would still be gone, but there would be people around him who loved him. There was Alice, for a start— Emily's sister. And Alice's husband, Jack. Reg had said how they'd all been friends together. They were there, and he wouldn't be on his own anymore. I put my drink down and faced him.

"Someone told me something a while ago, Reg. It didn't make much sense to me at the time, but I think it does now," I said. "It was about a brick."

Reg stared at me. I tried to get what I wanted to say straight in my head. It was important that I got it right. I took a deep breath and began.

"This person told me that if you're going through a bad time in your life, it can sometimes feel like you're carrying a brick around in your pocket."

Reg blinked as I carried on.

"Some days that brick will feel so heavy in your pocket that you can barely move. Every step takes so much effort, and it can feel almost impossible to do anything."

Reg nodded his head slowly.

"But some days, Reg . . . some days you will still have that brick in your pocket, but you won't even notice it. It'll always be there, but sometimes it won't feel as heavy. Does that make any sense?"

He didn't say anything, but his eyes looked watery. I watched him for a moment, and then I dropped my head. I thought I had said the right thing, but the story Dad had told me about the brick sounded silly when I said it out loud. I took another deep breath and looked back up at him.

"Reg, I need you to concentrate as I tell you something. I'm going to tell you how to get home. How to get home to the people you love. Then, if you feel the time is right, you can go back to the exact moment you left. Do you understand?"

He nodded.

"Right," I said, sitting forward on my chair. "You know the wooden egg in the cabinet?" I said.

And then I told him.

CHAPTER 45
SCIENCE

Charlie and I started going to science club on Fridays after school. I really didn't want to go at first, as the only time I'd ever stayed late at school was for detention and it seemed weird staying late out of choice. But Charlie gave me one of his looks, so I promised to give it a try.

Science club turned out to be brilliant. Charlie was right. You got to do really cool experiments like firing rockets using old bottles, vinegar, and baking soda.

One Friday we walked home after science club, and Charlie tried to explain something about the speed of sound to me. I wasn't really sure what he was talking about, but I nodded and tried to keep up. It was interesting to start with, but I couldn't grasp it all in my head. I think he must have realized I was struggling because he gave up.

"Maybe I'll tell you about it all another day, eh?" he said, and I smirked.

"Sorry, Charlie. My head is still full of stuff from science club. I don't think I can fit anything else in it."

He smiled at me. "I'm glad we sorted everything out between us," he said. "You're all right now, you know? You're not angry all the time like you used to be."

I nodded back but didn't say anything.

"*And* you've stopped calling me Charlie Geek, so that's a bonus, too," he said. "Anyway, see ya later, Maxwell."

And then he turned and headed off toward his home.

I turned down Reg's road. I usually popped in to see him on a Friday, but I wasn't going to stay long as it was getting late. Before school this morning, Mum had suggested we have a pizza-and-film night, just me and her, as Bex was going for a sleepover at Maddy's. I told her I'd like that.

I walked in through Reg's kitchen door like I always did and switched on the kettle.

"Only me, Reg! Do you want a cup of tea?" I shouted through to the living room.

There was no answer, but I got his mug out of the cupboard and put a tea bag in it anyway.

"Mum said would you like to come to our house for lunch on Sunday?" I called. "She thought you might like to . . ."

I walked into the living room and stopped. Reg's armchair was empty.

"Reg?" I went to the hallway and checked his bedroom and the bathroom. He wasn't anywhere.

"Reg? Where are you?" I called again.

The kettle in the kitchen clicked off, and the boiling water rumbled on for a few seconds and then stopped.

I looked around the living room and spotted a piece of folded paper propped up against his portrait. On it was one word in shaky handwriting.

Maxwell

I picked up the sheet and slowly opened it.

Thank you for everything, Maxwell.
It's time I went home.
Reg

I took a deep breath in the silence, and then I folded up the note and put it into my back pocket.

I walked over to the cabinet. The doors were open and the egg was there, lying beside the black hat. I closed the cabinet doors, then went into the kitchen and put Reg's mug back in the cupboard next to the tin of cookies.

I opened the side door and shivered as I stepped out into the cold air. I turned to take a final look at the bungalow I'd come to know so well. I smiled to myself.

"Bye, Reg," I said. And then I closed the door and headed home.

ABOUT THE AUTHOR

Lisa Thompson is the acclaimed author of *The Goldfish Boy* and *The Light Jar*. She has worked as a radio broadcast assistant—first at the BBC and then for an independent production company—making plays and comedy programs. During this time, she got to make tea for lots of famous people. She lives in Suffolk, England, with her family. Find her online at lisathompsonauthor.com and on Twitter at @lthompsonwrites.